LOVE ON THE REBOUND

HAWAII BILLIONAIRE ROMANCE SERIES

JENNIFER YOUNGBLOOD

SANDRA POOLE

ARBOR
HOUSE

GET YOUR FREE BOOK

Get Beastly Charm: A Contemporary retelling of beauty & the beast
for as a welcome gift when you sign up for my newsletter. You'll get

information on my new releases, book recommendations, discounts, and other freebies.

Sign up at jenniferyoungblood.com

PROLOGUE

Everly turned her face to the sun, liking how the warmth stretched her skin, making it feel tingly and tight. It was mid-afternoon, and the gentle rocking of the boat was lulling her to sleep. Mitchell shifted on the blanket and then angled toward her. Lightly, he trailed the tips of his fingers up and down her arm.

"What do you say we go for a dive before we head into shore?"

A lazy haze had settled over Everly, and all she wanted to do was sleep. "Maybe later," she mumbled.

"Come on," he urged. "Just once more, you know you want to." He leaned over and started tickling her.

She sat up, laughing. "Mitchell! Stop!"

"Come diving with me." His blue eyes were as clear as the sparkling water surrounding them. He thrust out his lower lip in a pout. "Please."

"Okay," she relented.

He flashed a dazzling smile. "Perfect! I'll help you get suited up."

Minutes later, they plunged into the water. Everly could feel the weight of the water pressing around her as they descended lower into the mysterious world below. Mitchell loved diving, but from the moment she'd entered the water she felt vulnerable. There were so many things that could go wrong, even for experienced divers. She tried to stay close to Mitchell as they explored.

Time was distorted underwater, but Everly was certain they'd been under too long. She kept pointing to the surface, shining like the moon overhead in the blue abyss. She tried to persuade Mitchell to go up with her. But he shook his head *no* and took off in another direction. She went after him. But as soon as she got close enough to touch him, he escaped her grasp, like a fish playing a game of tag. Finally, she couldn't handle it any longer. She started going up. Then she realized Mitchell was struggling. In a flurry, she went back down to help him. His eyes radiated panic through the mask. He was running out of air! She tried to help, but it was no use. Anguish wrenched her gut as she watched him sink into the black nothingness. Then Everly realized she was running out of air. She fought her way to the surface, trying to gulp in what little air her oxygen tank provided.

She couldn't breathe! A steel band was squeezing her lungs. She jerked to a sitting position and opened her eyes. It took Everly a second to realize where she was—in her bedroom, her cheeks wet with tears.

"Mommy?" Jordan scampered toward her. "I'm scared."

Had she cried out in her sleep and woken him up? She rubbed her eyes and tried to orient herself to the present as she patted the empty space beside her on the bed. "Come here."

He climbed into bed with her.

Everly lay back down and pulled up the covers as Jordan huddled next to her. The terror on Mitchell's face had felt so real. A shudder went through her. It had been a few months since she had the nightmare, and she'd hoped she'd finally moved beyond the trauma. It must've been brought on by the anxiety of getting ready for the trip tomorrow. She lay there, staring unseeingly at the ceiling, her mind lost in another time. Jordan's warm body was comforting. As she listened to his steady breathing, she finally drifted back to sleep.

1

Conflicting emotions churned in Everly's gut as she clutched Jordan's hand and began walking in the direction of the baggage claim. On the one hand, she was happy to be spending Christmas in Hawaii with Jordan ... away from the hectic hustle and bustle of her everyday life ... and away from the long arm of Roland and his cronies. On the other hand, she dreaded what she might find here.

From the moment she received the disturbing call from Benny Kai, a private investigator, looking into her late husband Mitchell's death, Everly instinctively knew she could only gain true peace by eventually coming here. Benny claimed there was a man living on the island whom he suspected to be Mitchell. He asked Everly to send him a picture of Mitchell for verification and promised he would call her back as soon as he received it. She never heard from him again. She called Benny back at the number he'd called her from. But she wasn't able to leave a message because his voicemail was full. Everly called a few more times until she finally got a recording telling her the number had been disconnected. Not knowing what else to do, she Googled Benny and came across the website for his business. She called the number listed, but it was also disconnected. The frustrating part was that she'd been so shocked by Benny's call that she'd not thought to ask the name of the man he presumed to be her deceased husband. So, she had nothing to go on. The whole thing was absurd. She wouldn't have given any credence to it whatsoever, but her best friend DeAnna swore up and down that she saw Mitchell at a restaurant in Honolulu while on vacation.

Five years ago, Mitchell went scuba diving with a work associate and friend in Lake Tahoe. They were on the lake's west side, near Rubicon Point, in an area where the lake plunges 1600 feet or more. As the pair began their ascent, Mitchell experienced difficulty with his equipment and began sinking. Paul, his companion, tried to help but was running out of air and had to resurface. Mitchell's body was never found. Coming to terms with the death of her husband had been grueling, especially without the closure of his remains. For months, Everly half-expected Mitchell to walk through the door any minute. When Jordan was born, she poured her heart and soul into him, and that helped ease the pain. But she was still having those wretched nightmares, where she was in the lake with Mitchell, watching him plunge to his death.

During those torturous months when she was grieving Mitchell's death, his business partner Roland Watson had been her rock. He was solicitous and kind, coming to her aid whenever she needed him. More importantly, Roland took an interest in Jordan. Everly and Roland's relationship developed until marriage was the next logical step. At first, their marriage had been idyllic, at first. He legally adopted Jordan and treated him as his own child. Everly thought life gave her a second chance at happiness, until she discovered that Roland was having multiple affairs. Again, her world came crashing down. She went through a heart-wrenching divorce that granted Roland visitation rights to see Jordan. Roland was an influential attorney in Charleston, South Carolina. There were few things he couldn't get. He kept close tabs on Everly and Jordan, to the point of stalking and determinedly ran off every possible suitor that came near her. Just when she felt the situation was pushing her to the breaking point, she got the call from Benny telling her Mitchell might still be alive.

Everly's first impulse was to drop everything and fly to Oahu that minute, but that wasn't possible. She had responsibilities—a demanding full-time job, her five-year-old son, and a mama with cancer to look after. Her mama Florence needed Everly to take her to weekly radiation and chemotherapy treatments. The day after Everly received Benny Kai's call, her mama was hospitalized for two weeks due to her weakened condition. Miraculously, Florence survived treatment and was now in remission. So, several months later, Everly decided to visit Hawaii during the holidays.

What did she hope to find here? Closure, maybe? Was Mitchell still alive? Had he been living another life all these years? It took her years to come to terms with his death, and now? Now she felt betrayed ... angry. If Mitchell faked his death, that meant he deserted her ... left her alone to fend for herself while she was pregnant. And it also meant she'd married two losers. She didn't even want to contemplate what that said about her judgment, or lack thereof. It was, surprisingly, much easier thinking of Mitchell as dead. She cringed. Had she really just thought that? Odds were that Mitchell did die in that diving accident. Poor Mitchell, here she was desecrating his memory. At any rate, the bottom line was—regardless of whether Mitchell was dead or alive, she no longer loved him. Of that she was sure. Her love for him died many years ago. The two of them started having problems a few months after their marriage, and things worsened when she became pregnant with Jordan. Still, she had a hard time believing he'd fake his death and assume another life.

Jordan tugged on her hand. "Mommy, I'm hungry."

Like most boys, Jordan was a bottomless pit. He'd eaten two packs of airline pretzels and one pack of cookies just before landing. Yet, she wasn't the least bit surprised that he was still hungry.

"Let's get our luggage. I've got some granola bars in my suitcase."

He frowned. "But my tummy hurts," he said, eyeing a nearby food stand.

The fragrant smell of teriyaki chicken wafted through the air making Everly's mouth water, reminding her that Jordan wasn't the only one who hungry.

"It won't take us long to get the luggage. Remember what we talked about? I need you to be a big boy, okay?"

He blew out a breath. "Okay." He switched gears. "When can we go to the beach? I want to build a sandcastle."

The excitement in Jordan's voice made her smile. He was a bundle of energy, and the only time he slowed down was when he was asleep. But he'd captured her heart the moment he was born—the best thing that had come from her marriage to Mitchell. "First thing in the morning, I promise."

He scrunched his nose. "Aw, man," he said slumping his shoulders in an exaggerated manner only a five-year-old could perfect. "I wanna do it today." He scrunched his eyebrows together. "Please?"

"We still have to get our rental car and drive to our place. It'll be dark by the time we get there." As she watched disappointment cloud his features she softened. "Hey, maybe we can find a pizza place. Would you like that?"

He brightened. "Pepperoni?"

"Of course."

He started skipping along beside her. Everly wished she had a tenth of Jordan's energy. Of course, it helped that he'd slept on the plane. But, she didn't. She could sleep in a car just fine. But, the moment that plane lifted off the ground she was wide-awake thinking about the empty air beneath her feet. The journey was starting to catch up with her. Her legs felt heavy, and the straps of her backpack cut into her shoulders. Everly's oversized bag felt like lead slung over her arm. Her day started at 4 a.m. when she hustled Jordan out of bed before driving to the airport in Charleston. From there they flew to Atlanta, followed by a 10-hour flight here. A soft bed and pillow sounded divine, but they still had a ways to go. According to Google Maps, it would take over an hour to get to their rental house on the North Shore. She'd booked a one-bedroom, one-bath cottage directly on Sunset Beach. Everly wanted a true Hawaiian experience, away from the touristy hotels. Plus, it would be easier to maintain a low profile, while checking into Mitchell.

Humidity pressed around Everly like a warm blanket as they walked by sections of walls, open to the outdoors, revealing lush green grass, palm trees, and bushes loaded with large, red hibiscus flowers. Coming from South Carolina, Everly was used to her share of humidity, but not this much. The sweet scent of plumeria flowers filled her senses as they passed a lei stand.

"Mommy, look!" Jordan exclaimed, pointing at the neat strands of white and pink flowers.

A pretty Polynesian girl in her mid-twenties smiled. "Aloha."

Everly returned the smile. "Aloha." She turned to Jordan, "The flowers are beautiful, aren't they?"

He nodded, his bright-blue eyes wide with wonderment.

For the first time since they'd left South Carolina, Everly felt a twinge of excitement. It would be nice to soak up some sun. Dig her toes into the sand on the beach. Feel the salty breeze on her face. Play in the ocean and build sandcastles with Jordan. Tomorrow, she planned on spending most of the day on the beach. Eventually, she'd have to search for Mitchell, but she planned to put that off for a few days. She and Jordan needed some R&R. A little downtime to steel her for whatever she'd find.

Everly's heart clutched when she saw a familiar face at baggage claim. Hot anger suffused through her as she glared at the man standing two carousels away. A panicked look came over him when he realized he'd been spotted. He ducked back and disappeared into the crowd. Everly's first impulse was to charge after the man, but she couldn't very well leave Jordan standing in the airport alone. What was his name? She searched her memory? Briggs. Yes, that was it. He was on her ex-husband's payroll. She'd seen him lurking around Roland's office. She should've known Roland would have her followed.

"Ouch!" Jordan yelped. "You're squeezing my hand."

"Oh, honey. I'm sorry." She relaxed her grip. Dread settled in the center of her stomach. Would she ever be able to escape Roland?

Panic steamrolled over her. She'd tried to be discreet about her travel plans. She didn't even tell Jordan about their trip until they arrived at the airport, fearing he'd tell Roland. She'd not breathed a word to her co-workers at the fitness center. Only her mama knew. Everly only planned to be gone for two weeks. Two measly weeks! And Roland sent his guy all the way here to watch her. A cold sweat broke over her brow. Had Roland somehow gotten wind that she was looking for Mitchell? Did he have a tracker on her phone? Was he having her followed 24/7? She didn't know whether to laugh or cry. Roland had a different woman on his arm nearly every week, and yet, he was insanely jealous about her. It was crazy! She glanced around, trying to catch sight of the man, but he was nowhere to be found. Even so, she knew he was nearby ... watching.

2

It was a perfect morning on the beach. Everly looked up at the sky, dotted with puffy, white clouds and across the ocean that expanded seamlessly into the distant horizon. The water with its patches of turquoise, mixed with gray and white, reminded her of a giant quilt where the edges attempted to cover the sand. Just when it managed to get a good grip, it got yanked back, only to repeat the same motion again. A gust of wind whipped hair into her mouth. She gathered it into a ponytail and held it up off her neck. There was something awesome about being in the midst of the perpetual motion of churning water, rocks, and sand. Out here, she could almost forget about her problems. *Almost* being the operative word. She'd hardly slept a wink the night before, thinking of Roland and how he'd sent his man to follow her. She scowled as she placed her hand above her eyes as a shield and scoured the surrounding area. Was Briggs here now ... watching them? A shiver shimmied down her spine, as she shook off the depressing thought. She would not let Roland ruin this day. Jordan was busily constructing a sandcastle village, his cherubic face a picture of determination, blonde hair flapping happily in the wind.

Her eyes followed a man and little girl as they walked from one of the nearby houses and occupied the space about twenty feet to her right. Her breath caught. The guy was immaculately gorgeous—tall with sinewy muscles that moved like a well-oiled machine under his bronze skin. He was wearing sunglasses, and his hair, closely cropped on the sides, was thick and curly on top. A large beach bag and chairs were slung over one shoulder. She watched as he deposited the bag onto the sand and commenced setting up two camp chairs and spreading a blanket over the sand. The little girl was about Jordan's age. Her dark hair was pulled into a high ponytail. Her bright pink bathing suit accentuated her brown skin. When the guy removed his shirt, Everly's throat went dry. Wow! Was he real? Decorum dictated she look away, but she couldn't seem to make herself do it. There was something familiar about the man. What was it? It pricked at her mind, but she couldn't figure out where she'd seen him before. At that moment, he noticed her attention. A corner of his mouth lifted, and he gave her a friendly nod. She offered a tight smile in response. How embarrassing! He'd felt her watching him. Quickly, she looked away and focused her attention on Jordan. Amusement bubbled over her chagrin. It was nice to know that despite the trauma she'd experienced with the previous two men in her life, she could still find one attractive. She couldn't remember the last time she'd taken time out of her busy schedule to notice a man, much less gawk at him. A fact made more impressive by her working at a fitness center where men paraded around like roosters, flexing their biceps. Maybe Hawaii was lowering her inhibitions? Or, mowing them over flat. Geez! Was she that starved for male attention? Besides, he was probably married. He did have his daughter with him. Then again, she had her son with her, and she wasn't married.

Everly's phone buzzed. She retrieved it from her purse and frowned. It was Roland. Fresh anger sizzled through her. Should she answer it? He'd already called five or six times this morning, but she'd let it go to voicemail. Even as she thought the words, she slid her finger across the face of the phone, answering it. She couldn't avoid him forever, and refused to be bullied by him.

"Hello," she said tersely.

"Hey, babe." Roland's voice was smooth like the glassy sand nearest the water. "How are things?"

"Fine." She sat silently, waiting for him to respond.

"Listen, we haven't discussed this, but I would really like to spend Christmas day with you and Jordan ... and, of course, your mom's welcome to join us."

Roland, master of mind games. She squinted in irritation. "No, that won't be possible. I have other plans."

"That's too bad." Long pause. "I'm taking a few days off work. Maybe I can stop by this afternoon and take Jordan out for some ice cream."

It was sickening to hear him carrying on as if he didn't know she was 5,000 miles away. "Cut the crap, Roland. I saw your boy last night."

Longer pause followed by a nervous laugh. "Guess I can't fool you, can I, hon?" His voice took on an edge. "You know, you could've just told me you were going to Hawaii for Christmas. Jordan's my son. I have a legal right to know where he is."

Roland liked to throw around his legal weight, reminding her he held all the cards. Keeping her voice light, she replied. "Oh? I thought you knew I was coming here."

"No, I didn't. Like I said, I'm taking a few days off. I can hop a plane and be there in a few hours."

Panic ignited through her as she forced a laugh. "And I suppose you'll bring your latest girlfriend ... what's her name? I'm sorry, but there've been so many, I can't keep track of them."

"Babe, those girls mean nothing to me. I only care about you and Jordan. You know I'll always look after you."

The veiled threat stabbed like an ice pick through her heart, chilling her to the core. "It's not necessary for you to come here. Jordan and I are taking a short vacation. We'll be back in two weeks. And that's that. Thanks for calling, but I've gotta go. See ya." She ended the call before he could say anything else.

Her phone buzzed. Roland, again! She silenced it and gazed at the horizon. With Roland's man stuck to her like glue, it was going to be nearly impossible to find out about Mitchell. A new thought entered her head. If Mitchell were indeed alive, perhaps she could persuade him to help her escape Roland's clutches. It was a long shot, but it offered a glimmer of hope.

"Excuse me." She gulped when she looked up to see Mr. Perfect, standing over her. He smiled, revealing even, white teeth. "I was wondering if I could use some of your sun block for my niece. I ran out." He held up an empty bottle.

His voice was just husky enough to titillate her senses. She'd heard of women turning to mush at the sight of muscled, Polynesian men, and now she knew why. Then again, upon closer look, he looked to be of mixed heritage. He wasn't bulky, but tall and lean, his muscles in perfect proportion to his frame. It took effort to keep her eyes fixed on his sunglasses rather than his rock-hard abs and pecs. Her clients at the club would kill for a body like his.

Luckily, before she could make a complete imbecile of herself, she managed to find her voice. "Of course." She rummaged around in the bottomless pit of her bag, searching for the sun block. "Here you go," she said, holding it up like it was the prize catch of the day.

"Thanks." He reached for it. "You have a lovely accent. Where are you from?"

"Charleston, South Carolina." She cocked her head, studying him. "You got that from only two sentences? Impressive."

He chuckled. "Well, you do stand out. It's not every day I hear a Southern twang on the island." The little girl came running up to his side. She tugged on his hand. "Uncle, can I help build sandcastles with him?" She pointed at Jordan.

"Is that all right with you?" the guy said, turning to Everly.

Uncle ... so she wasn't his daughter. She was a cutie. And so polite. "Yes, I think Jordan would like that. What's your name?" Everly asked.

She looked down at the ground.

He put a hand on her shoulder. "Tell her," he prompted.

"Sadie," she said shyly.

Everly gave her an encouraging look. "That's a pretty name."

Sadie smiled broadly.

"I'm Everly and that's my son Jordan." She looked over to where he was playing. "Jordan, this is Sadie. She's going to help you build sandcastles."

"Okey dokey artichokey," Jordan chimed.

Sadie sniggered at his joke and went to play with him.

"Everly," the man said, giving her an appraising look. "It suits you."

"Thanks."

"I'm Christian." He motioned at the spot beside her chair. "Do you mind if I join you?"

"Not at all." She thought he might fetch one of his chairs, but he sat down on the sand and drew up his knees, clasping his arms around them.

"I'm sorry, I only brought one chair."

"No problem. I don't mind sitting on the sand."

Her chair sat low-to-the-ground, so that they were almost eye level.

"I'm assuming you're here on vacation?"

"Yes, Jordan and I are staying a couple of weeks."

"Oh, so you're spending Christmas here?"

"Yes."

"Is it just the two of you?"

"Yes." She bit back a smile. His ring finger was bare, and he was fishing about her status. She glanced at his strong, clean jaw line, which had a sexy layer of stubble. She was itching to know what he looked like underneath his sunglasses. Then she realized she was also wearing sunglasses. Glad she took the time to put on eyeliner and mascara, she nonchalantly lifted her sunglasses, placing them on her head. She glanced down at her black, two-piece swimsuit, making sure to suck in her stomach. Even though she was physically in the best shape she'd ever been, it was hard to not feel inferior compared to his chiseled physique.

"Ah, the woman behind the glasses." A smile lifted the corners of his mouth. "You look exactly as I imagined."

Was that a good or bad thing? She waited for him to elaborate, but he didn't. Nor did he remove his glasses. "Are you and Sadie here on vacation?"

"No, we live here." He pointed toward the houses behind them. "My sister Kat lives just over there."

"I see." She was suddenly curious to know more about him. "Do you watch Sadie often?"

He shrugged. "I help out when I can. Kat's in the hotel business, and she travels a lot. She's also a single mom, so Sadie spends a lot of time with me."

She nodded, about to ask what he did for a living, but he spoke first. "Tell me about yourself ... are you married?"

His bluntness was refreshing. She chuckled. "Not anymore. How about you?"

The pleased look on his face caused her insides to warm. "Nope. No wife. It's just me."

Unsure how to respond, she just nodded.

"What do you do for a living, Everly?"

"I'm a fitness trainer. I manage a fitness center and facilitate a training program for employees of several corporations."

"Impressive. No wonder you're so fit."

Her cheeks flushed. "Thanks," she mumbled. She wished again to see his eyes, to get a read on him. It was hard to get a feel for who he really was underneath the sunglasses. Then again, it really didn't matter because she'd probably never see him again. And it was for the best. Her life was complicated enough as it was. Christian lived in Hawaii, a world away from her. Her ex-husband was a jealous maniac, and there was a small chance, the husband she thought was dead was still alive and living on the island. Still, it was nice, sitting on the beach, of one of the most beautiful places in the world, talking to this drop-dead gorgeous man who seemed interested in her. "What do you do for a living?"

He shifted uncomfortably, and she got the feeling she'd asked the wrong question. Without thinking, she touched his arm. "Are you okay?"

He gave her a strained smile. "Yeah." He let out a breath before removing his sunglasses and placing them on his head.

She found herself staring into his very recognizable turquoise eyes. She gasped. "You're Christian Ross! I thought you looked familiar, but I couldn't place you ... until you removed the sunglasses." Christian was one of the biggest actors in Hollywood, starring in a string of blockbuster action movies. She searched her brain. What were the most famous ones called? They were some of Roland's favorites, so she'd watched them with him a number of times, when they were married. "*Freefall, Crossfire* and ..."

"*Lethal Target,*" he finished for her.

"Yeah, that's right, *Lethal Target*. But those came out a few years ago. What have you been in recently?"

He rubbed his jaw. "I'm semi-retired."

"Oh, it must be nice." She regretted her words the instant she saw the crease between his brows.

"I suppose," he huffed.

A wall went up between them. She was confused for a second, then remembered ... a snippet she'd read in a magazine while getting her hair done at the beauty salon. Something about a car accident, and his girlfriend who'd been injured. No wonder he suddenly withdrew. "I'm sorry. I didn't mean to touch a nerve."

Pain flickered over his handsome face. "It's okay."

"That's why you kept your sunglasses on, isn't it? So I wouldn't recognize you."

"Yes," he admitted. "It's nice to talk to someone and just be me. Not Christian Ross the actor, just plain, old me. No expectations. No judgment."

"I get it." Even as she spoke the words Everly's mind was whirling. She was sitting on a beach with Christian Ross! It took all the effort she could summon to keep a passive expression on her face as she sought for something to say that didn't revolve around acting. "So, Christian," she drawled, laying her accent on super thick, "considering I'm from South Carolina. And seeing how this is my first time in Hawaii. Tell me ... what do you do for fun around here?"

He didn't miss a beat. "You mean something other than going to the beach, trying to pick up on unsuspecting southern belles who're willing to share their sun block with a complete stranger?"

She chuckled. "Yeah, something other than that."

He scratched his head. "Hmm ... let's see. I grew up surfing and playing football. I like to garden. And I've been training for an Ironman."

"An Ironman? Wow! No wonder you look like you do." Her face flamed when she realized what she'd said. "Um ... I mean that's why you're in such good shape."

His eyes twinkled in amusement, thoroughly enjoying her discomfort. He winked. "Thanks."

Sadie let out a cry and then started bawling. Christian leapt to his feet and rushed to her side. "What's wrong?"

Everly also stood and walked to where Jordan and Sadie were playing.

Sadie pointed an accusing finger at Jordan. "He threw sand in my eyes!"

Christian's face turned a shade darker. "What?"

Everly looked at Jordan in disbelief. "Did you throw sand at Sadie?"

Jordan's lower lip trembled. "I didn't mean to."

"How could you do that?" Christian demanded.

Jordan erupted into tears. "I-it was an accident," he stammered. "I was digging out a big rock. It was hard to get around it, and the sand came up." He looked at Everly with pleading eyes. "I'm sorry, Mommy. I'm sorry!"

Sadie rubbed her eyes, wailing. "It burns!"

Everly rushed over to her bag and grabbed a bottle of water. Then she darted back. "Flush her eyes with this."

Christian cupped his hands, and Everly poured water into them. He splashed the water into Sadie's eyes. All the while, she screamed. Everly poured more water into Christian's hands, and he repeated the process. Finally, Sadie stopped wailing but was still crying in soft gulps.

Anger twisted over Christian's face as he glared at Jordan. "This is unacceptable. You were being a menace."

For a second, Everly didn't think she'd heard him correctly. A menace? Had he really just said that? She bristled like a soaked cat. "How dare you pass judgment on my son, when you don't know the first thing about him. He said it was an accident."

He let out an incredulous laugh. "And you believe him?"

She squared her shoulders, looking Christian in the eye. "Yes, I do." She turned to Jordan. "Now, apologize to Sadie."

Jordan shook his head *no* and buried it in Everly's waist. "I didn't mean to hurt her," he cried.

"Jordan," she said firmly, attempting to extricate him from her waist, "even though it was an accident, you still need to apologize."

Christian shot her a blistering look. "I believe he's done enough."

She rocked back. What a jerk! Par for the course. She should've known Christian was too good to be true. "Yep, I believe you're right," she snapped. "Let's go!"

Jordan drew back from her, his eyes wide. "But I wanna stay at the beach."

"We're leaving ... now!"

Jordan melted into tears. "Please, Mommy. Let's stay. I didn't mean to hurt Sadie. I promise, I didn't."

Everly's cheeks stung from the heat of embarrassment as she turned her back on him and started shoving the sand toys into the bag. Jordan threw himself down on the sand and started squalling like he was dying. She glanced at Christian, who looked amused. When he chuckled, her anger rose to new heights. Her hand flew to her hip, and she thrust out her chest, ready to spar. "You know what you can do, Mr. High and Mighty! You can take your stupid grin and stick it where the sun don't shine!"

Christian's jaw dropped.

She stomped over to where she'd been sitting and packed everything away in record time. Jordan was still making a show of crying, but it was obvious from his whiny tone that his heart wasn't in it. Christian and Sadie just stood there, watching. Of all the times for

Jordan to pitch a fit! Why did it have to be now? Everly wanted to wipe that smug expression off Christian's face and shove him head-first into the sand.

"Let's go, Jordan," she commanded in her most authoritative voice. Any other time, she would've simply picked him up and carried him, despite the kicking and screaming, but she couldn't because her hands were loaded with beach paraphernalia. She could tell from the look on Jordan's face he was determined to make this a power struggle. He knew she was humiliated and wanted to leave quickly. She gave him a steely look. "I'm leaving. Unless you want to be left out here alone, I suggest you come too."

Christian was surprised. "You're just going to leave him here?"

She glanced at Jordan, who was hanging on every word. The only way to establish clear boundaries was to press forward. "It's his choice. Leave with me now or stay here alone." She winced inwardly. This could end badly. There was no way she was going to leave Jordan out here alone; but now that she'd said it, she had to at least try and follow through. She turned on her heel and began walking toward the beach house. When Jordan finally got up and trudged along behind her, she was relieved.

So much for a day of R&R at the beach!

3

"I'm sorry, man. I've given it a lot of thought, and I'm just not up to doing another Jase Scott movie right now." Christian gripped the phone, preparing himself for the backlash that was sure to follow. Not only was Boston Andrews his agent, but also a close friend. Boston ran a talent agency in L.A. and started representing Christian years ago, when he first went into acting. The two weathered their fair share of storms in the cutthroat, Hollywood industry before attaining unprecedented success when Christian landed the leading role of Jase Scott in the wildly popular action series about a rogue CIA Agent. From the moment Christian first read the screenplay, he knew he was a shoo-in for the role. And as an added bonus, he was able to do his own stunts. *Freefall*, the first movie in the series, had catapulted him to stardom overnight. After *Lethal Target* and *Crossfire* came out, he soared to the top of the A-List, becoming a Hollywood favorite, akin to the caliber of Tom Cruise and Robert Downey, Jr. The amount of money he was paid per movie was staggering, which is why Boston had been begging him to do another.

"You're killing me, dude," Boston lamented. "You told me you were up for this one, so I made commitments."

The reason Boston was one of the most successful agents in L.A.

was because he rarely took *no* for an answer. But no amount of goading was going to persuade Christian to go back to that dog-eat-dog world. "I told you, I'd think about it," Christian countered, "and I have. But it's not gonna happen."

Boston swore under his breath. "The entire film's scheduled to be shot in Georgia, due to all the state film credits. You won't even have to step foot in L.A."

"What about the PR campaign? And the premiere?"

Pregnant pause. "Yeah ... there may be a little of that, but we can work around your schedule."

Christian rolled his eyes. "Heard that one before."

"Look, man. I know you're still dealing with crud from the accident ... and Heather's death, but it's been three years. You can't hide out forever. Sooner or later, you're gonna have to face it."

Christian reached for the empty juice can on the table beside him and crushed it in his fist. "You have no idea what you're talking about. I'm not hiding out. This is my home. I grew up here, remember?"

"I get that, but acting's in your blood. You lived for it before ... I just want to see you happy."

"And, make a few million off the deal."

"That hurt, man. I'm only trying to make a living. Unlike you, I don't have a brainiac sister who can work her magic and turn my millions into billions."

Christian's neck and shoulders tightened. Every conversation with Boston felt like a thrashing. He loved the guy, but he was exhausting. "The acting has never been about the money for me," he said flatly.

"Spoken like someone with an endless supply of it." When Christian remained silent, Boston continued. "Okay, we won't discuss the movie anymore today, but you should do the interview with *Introspective Magazine*. At least give me that ... for old time's sake."

Christian blew out a breath. Boston was backing him into a corner. He had a sneaking suspicion that was Boston's plan all along —to needle him about the movie, knowing he would say *no*, then hit him up for the interview. That was the problem with having a long-time friend—Boston knew just how to work him. "Okay," he relented. "When is it?"

"The day after Christmas."

"Seriously? You booked an interview during the holidays?"

"Oh, quit your blustering. Before you hit it big, you would've given your eyeteeth to have an interview with *Introspective*. The interviewer will come to you."

"No way! You know how I feel about that. I don't like anyone coming here. I'll meet the interviewer at a restaurant."

"Yeah ... right. And get bombarded by curious fans? I don't think so."

"Okay, I'll meet the interviewer at a hotel. I'll even pay for a private room. How's that?"

"Nope. Won't work."

Christian frowned. "Why not?"

"The segment's about celebrities in their homes."

"You're starting to push my buttons, Boston."

He chuckled. "Nah! Just doing my job. All right." He paused. "I've got another call coming in. Better let you go."

"I see how it is ... you get what you want, and you're ready to end the call."

Boston laughed nervously. "Not everyone lives in paradise, my friend. Like I said earlier, some of us still work for a living."

"I hear ya," Christian said dryly.

"Gotta run, man. See ya."

Before Christian could say *bye*, Boston ended the call. Christian sighed heavily and placed his phone on the nearby table.

Same old Boston ... his nose to the grindstone 24/7. In many ways, he envied Boston. He had purpose ... something driving him. Not so long ago, Christian had been like that too, pouring himself into his roles, working dawn to dusk. Going to bed exhausted, then getting up the next day and doing it all over again. But he wasn't the same man he'd been before the accident and Heather's death. It had taken super human effort for him to put his life back together, and he couldn't go back to what he was before. His life at Pupukea Estate was quiet and ordered. And yes, some might call it boring, but he preferred to think of it as *peaceful*. His gaze took in the immaculately landscaped grounds with the ocean sparkling like diamonds in the distance. One of his favorite spots was right here, where he was sitting, beside the large, free-form pool nestled at the base of a breathtaking, man-made waterfall. The water, steadily cascading over the rocks, was therapeutic, helping to take the edge off his nerves. The estate was his world now, and he couldn't ... *wouldn't* go back to that other world. As a young boy, growing up poor in the nearby town of Laie, he never would've imagined he would one day have a home like this. His sister Kat bought a house on Sunset Beach and tried to talk him into doing the same, but he preferred to be in the mountains, where no one would bother him. It had taken him months to find the perfect location—remote, yet close enough to the ocean to give him an exquisite view. In fact, he was only about five miles from the beach, even though it felt like he was in an isolated location.

He looked at Sadie, playing in the shallow part of the pool, ten or so feet from where he was sitting.

"Uncle," she called when she realized he was looking at her. She pinched her nose. "Watch this!" she said, ducking her head under water.

When she came up, he clapped. "Very good." A broad smile stretched across her face. Sadie was learning to swim. In many ways, his sister Kat's frequent travels were a blessing, because they allowed him to spend so much time with Sadie. When looking after Sadie, he didn't focus as much on his own demons. This time, Kat went to the Bahamas to open up a new hotel. She'd get back tomorrow afternoon. It was hard to believe Christmas was only two days away. His stomach clenched. He'd always loved the holidays ... until Heather died on Christmas Eve. The last three years, Christmas brought back so many regrets and painful memories that he went on autopilot around Thanksgiving and simply got through the next month as best he could. Had it not been for Sadie, he wouldn't have even put up a tree. She'd talked incessantly about Santa Claus the past few weeks, and he'd used it as a bargaining chip to promote good behavior. He sighed heavily. All he had to do was survive the next two days, and he'd be okay.

His thoughts went to Everly and the sand fiasco. Everything had been going so well ... at first. Her charming accent captured him from the get-go, but it was more than that. He couldn't remember the last time he'd felt such a strong connection with someone. When she realized who he was, she didn't fawn over him like most women did. She just kept talking to him like he was a regular person. He kept picturing how flecks of gold sparkled in her hazel eyes when she smiled. And the way her thick mane of wavy hair framed her delicately sculpted features and rosy lips. It didn't hurt that she had an amazing figure. Her petite body was slender, yet toned. She had the beginnings of a tan, but it wasn't overdone like the majority of the women in Hollywood. More than anything, she felt genuine—the real deal, as opposed to the Photoshop version. And, he admired her grit, especially when the mother-bear in her came out, defending her son. Admittedly, he'd overreacted when Jordan threw sand in Sadie's eyes. And, if he had it to do over again, he wouldn't have been so accusatory. What was it she'd said to him? Something about "sticking his grin where the sun didn't shine." He chuckled.

"What's so funny?"

He looked up as Mele, his housekeeper and cook took the seat beside him. He and Mele had grown up in the same neighborhood, but they didn't have much interaction when they were younger because she was ten years older. She and her husband Jarin had three rowdy boys, so Mele could hold her own. Like many locals, she was a coconut—hard on the outside, but mushy and sweet on the inside. Half the time, she treated Christian like he was one of her sons. Mele jabbed him with her elbow. "Well?"

"Well what?" he said, rubbing his arm. "That hurt, by the way."

She fluffed her short hair with a sniff. "You were sitting there smiling like da mongoose that ate da rat. Just tell me, already. What's going on?"

"Nothing."

Her perceptive black eyes flickered over him. "You not getting out of this, brah. I've seen that look before. You met someone."

There wasn't much he could hide from Mele. "I did not," he protested, but couldn't hide the smile that broke over his lips.

She pointed. "Ah, I knew it. Who is she? Do I know her?"

"Nah, she's here on vacation."

Her face fell. "What? How long is she here for?"

"A coupla weeks."

She sighed heavily. "Well, at least you're showing some interest. I was beginning to wonder if ya gonna spend the rest of your life holed up here, licking your wounds."

"Hey, that's harsh."

"No, it da truth," she countered, clamping her lips together so forcefully that it caused her fleshy chin to jiggle. Then her eyes grew soft around the edges. "I'm glad you found someone."

He held up his hands. "Whoa! I only met her today. Don't go marrying me off just yet."

She laughed. "What's her name?"

"Everly."

"Hmm ... I like it. Is she pretty?"

"Of course she's pretty."

"When do I get to meet her?"

Before Christian could answer, a loud siren rent the air, causing the hair on his neck to lift. Fear licked through Mele's eyes as she grabbed his arm. "Oh, no. Is that what I think it is?"

Christian's mouth went dry as he nodded. Then he reached for his phone and tapped on the Internet app to check the weather. Sadie scampered out of the pool and ran to them, her hands pressed over her ears. Mele placed a towel around her.

"Do you think it's a test?" Mele asked.

Christian glanced at the strip of ocean in the distance. "Tests are done at the beginning of the month, and they don't last this long."

"It hurts my ears," Sadie said, wrinkling her nose as she drew her chin into her neck like a turtle trying to escape into its shell.

A minute later, Christian's lips formed a grim line. "According to this report, there's been an earthquake in Canada. A tsunami's headed right for us."

Tears pooled in Mele's eyes as she placed her hands over her mouth. "I've got to call Jarin. He's got to get the boys to higher ground. How long have we got?"

"According to this report, about five hours."

CHAPTER 4

Everly was so bent-out-of-shape after the beach incident it took her over an hour to calm down. Unable to get Christian off her mind, she pulled out her laptop and Googled him. The first images she found showed him on the red carpet at a movie premiere, smiling and waving at the camera, a blonde bombshell draped over his arm. It didn't take long to find more—the news report outlining the car accident that left his girlfriend paralyzed from the waist down. And then a few months later, the girl took her own life. Everly felt a wave of compassion for him. It was grueling to lose Mitchell in a freak diving accident, but for the most part, she'd been able to deal with the pain privately. She couldn't imagine how hard it must've been for Christian to have his personal tragedy plastered all over the media for the world to see. Looking at him, it was hard to believe he'd experienced a minute's worth of hardship. As far as outward appearances went, the Christian she met on the beach embodied the superstar actor who radiated confidence. But she knew from experience that tragedy left a scar, not easily erased. It just went to show, no one is above heartache. Her mama always said, "If you think someone else has the perfect life, then you should clean your glasses and look again."

Admittedly, it was a little hard to stay peeved at Christian after reading about those tragic events. Still, he had no right to treat Jordan the way he had. She should've known from the moment Christian flashed his cocky grin that he was trouble. She drew the wrong sort of guy as sure as bees attract honey. It seemed to be in her DNA. Her mama had never been keen on Mitchell, but she held her tongue because she knew how much Everly loved him. When Roland came along, Mama was very vocal about her dislike for him. If only Everly had listened, it would've saved her a world of grief. Even now, 2 ½ years after the divorce, she was still trapped in Roland's treacherous web. There seemed to be no escaping his influence, even here, on this island.

The beach house was getting a little stuffy. She pulled at her shirt before going to open the scroll-out windows. Back home, she could've just turned on the air, but this house didn't have air conditioning. According to the instruction book from the owners, it wasn't necessary due to the constant breeze. As she opened the windows and yanked back the drapes, it occurred to her that Briggs might be watching. She glared out the window. If she caught sight of the wretched man, he was going to get a piece of her mind, by golly!

Jordan had been watching a movie on her iPad. The minute it was over, he placed it on the couch and bounced up and down. "Can we go back to the beach?"

The eager expression on his little face was so darn cute that if she hadn't already made other plans, she would've taken him. "We'll go to the beach tomorrow, okay?"

His face fell.

"We're going to a luau at the Polynesian Cultural Center. And then we're watching the night show."

He wrinkled his nose. "I don't want to go to the night show."

"Don't you want to see the guys twirling fire?" Heck. She wanted to see them. In high school, she was a majorette. The grand finale of the football season was when the majorettes twirled fire. The stadium lights were turned off, and the batons were lit. Of course, she only twirled a baton, whereas these guys twirled knives. It had been intimidating enough to twirl fire, much less knives.

Jordan clapped his hands. "I want to see the fire. Can we go now?"

"We have to get cleaned up first."

"Okay, Mommy."

Everly's heart jumped into her throat when she heard the ear-splitting sound of a siren.

"What's that?" Jordan said, wide-eyed.

"I—I'm not sure. But it can't be good," she mumbled, reaching for the TV remote. She flipped through the channels until she came to a local station. She broke out in a cold sweat, realizing what was happening. Her hands started to tremble.

Jordan tugged on her shirt. "Mommy? What's wrong?"

Panic tumbled over her as she bit into her lower lip. The grim-faced news anchor was telling people to evacuate to higher ground.

"If you get stuck in traffic, you need to leave your vehicle and proceed on foot. I repeat. Leave your vehicle, if necessary, and walk."

Her mind whirled as she tried to think. Where were they supposed to go? This trip was turning into a nightmare. She shuddered to think what would happen to them if a tsunami actually hit. Her thoughts raced to the 2004 tsunami that devastated Thailand the day after Christmas. She remembered it so vividly because her friend had been there on vacation with her parents. They were having breakfast at a resort when the deadly wave hit. Lynn was the only one of the three who survived.

Fear iced through Everly as she looked at Jordan, so innocent and vulnerable. She had an overwhelming need to protect him at all costs. But, how? For a second, she felt paralyzed, unsure what to do. She uttered a silent prayer for help and then forced herself to act.

"Mommy, I'm hungry," Jordan said from the backseat.

"I know, honey. We'll get something to eat soon."

"But I'm hungry!" he whined.

Everly fought to keep her voice even. "There's nothing I can do about it right now. Please just sit back, okay?" She gripped the steering wheel, panic boiling inside her as she glanced at the endless expanse of ocean on her right. What had looked so picturesque the day before was now a ticking time bomb, and they were stuck in grid-lock traffic. She kept expecting a wall of water to rush over them any minute. It had been over an hour since they left the beach house and they'd gone little more than a mile. The scene around them was chaos, with horns blaring and throngs of people walking beside the cars. Everly had tried to call the owners of the beach house to ask where she could go to reach safe ground, but no one answered. She was grateful she'd had the presence of mind to look up an evacuation map before darting out the door. From what she could tell, most of the people on foot were tourists that looked scared out of their minds.

According to the map, the closest place for them to go was up Pupukea Road. And according to the GPS, they were only a couple of miles away. But in this traffic, it could take them two or more hours just to reach the road. And then they had to go up it a few miles to get to the safe zone. People were walking faster than she was driving.

"My tummy hurts, Mommy. I'm hungry."

Jordan was asking for a snack when they left the house, but Everly was too keyed up to stop and give him something. The back-pack containing the food was in the backseat. There was no way to get to it while driving. To make matters worse, Jordan could sense her fear, growing larger by the minute. When she saw an empty space on the side of the road, she made a split-second decision. She pulled over so quickly on the shoulder of the road that the car behind her had to slam on the brakes to keep from plowing into the back of her. The man laid on his horn and shook his fist as he drove past.

"Sorry," she said absently, barely looking in his direction. She reached for her purse and slung it over her shoulder. Then she exited the car and rushed around to get Jordan. She'd put essentials in the backpack, in case they had to walk. At the time, however, she really didn't think it would come to that. But here they were. Unfortunately, she'd be forced to leave the remainder of their luggage locked in the trunk. If a tsunami hit, the car and the luggage would be obliterated.

The need to get Jordan and herself to safety was so consuming she could hardly breathe. She tried to regulate her breathing as she unbuckled Jordan from the car seat and took a firm hold on his hand.

"Are we going to the beach now?" he asked, looking eagerly at the ocean.

"No, but we're going to get you a snack." She reached for the backpack, unzipped it, and grabbed a pack of peanut butter crackers. She tore open the wrapper and handed them to Jordan. Then she shoved her purse into the backpack and put it on her shoulders. "Let's go."

Jordan looked at her like she'd lost her mind. "But, the car."

"The traffic's moving too slow. We need to walk." Her plan was to let Jordan walk as far as he could, then carry him the rest of the way. To Jordan's credit he made it about thirty minutes before he started whining, and they'd kept a pretty good pace.

"My feet hurt."

She picked him up and balanced him on her hip, hoping that a lifetime spent exercising would give her the stamina she needed to carry Jordan out of harm's way. Forty minutes later, her arm was throbbing, and she was covered in sweat. The shoulder of the road wasn't much of a shoulder at all. It was so rocky that she'd nearly turned her ankle a couple of times. And it was difficult to stay out of the way of the endless line of cars that were moving at a snail's pace. Thankfully, they were nearing Pupukea Road. She wanted to get as far from the coastline as she could. Her phone was buzzing, and she figured it was either her mama or Roland, checking to see if she and Jordan were okay. But she didn't have time to talk. Tears burned her eyes. Her strength was giving out. She put Jordan down and flexed her throbbing arm. The irony of her situation hit her full force as she looked at the hundreds of people around her, all fleeing for their lives. She was surrounded by people, and yet, she was totally alone.

She wiped her brow with the back of her hand. "Do you think you can walk a few minutes? Mommy's tired."

Jordan nodded.

"Good." She took his hand and pulled him along as fast as his little legs could go. They only got about ten minutes up the road, however, before Jordan started crying. She felt his pain, but they couldn't stop. "We have to keep going."

A man stepped up next to them, and her blood ran cold. Briggs!

Instinctively, she drew Jordan close, her eyes narrowing as she glared at the balding man, who was built like a linebacker. "What do you want?"

"I want to help you."

She let out a harsh laugh, not liking the way his cold eyes moved over her. She suspected fear of Roland was the only thing preventing him from making a pass at her. "You can help me, by leaving me alone."

He squared his jaw. "I don't think I can do that."

Fear rose thick in her throat. "You have no right to be here!"

"Roland has a right to know what's happening to his wife and child."

She straightened to her full height and looked Briggs in the eye. "For your information, Roland abdicated any right to me, the minute he took up with every harlot east of the Mississippi. And in case it escaped your pea-sized brain, there's a tsunami on its way." She gritted her teeth. "So, get out of my way."

She tried to barrel past him, but he blocked her way.

"You and the kid are coming with me! I promised Roland I would keep you safe."

A hysterical laugh escaped her throat. "Keep me safe? You? And just how in the heck do you expect to do that? Every minute I stand here, arguing with you, puts me and my son in greater danger." Jordan clutched her hand, tears bubbling in his eyes as he looked up at her.

"M—Mommy?"

Anger flared over her. "See what you did? You're scaring him!"

Brigg's face went flush. "I have a car parked nearby." He grabbed Everly's arm in a vice grip. She jerked, trying to escape. The motion caused Jordan to fall. When he started to cry, Everly had to push back her own angry tears. She helped Jordan to his feet. His knees and hands were scraped and bleeding.

"Let's go," Briggs barked, a ruthless expression on his face.

The last thing Everly wanted to do was get in the car with this thug. If she started screaming, would anyone come to her aid? It wasn't as if they had time to stop and help her. Not knowing what else to do, she uttered another silent prayer for help. And then she saw him striding towards them.

CHAPTER 5

"Is there a problem here?" Christian said.

Everly's knees went weak with relief. She'd never been so happy to see someone in her life. And she certainly hadn't expected her deliverance to come from the very man who'd consumed her thoughts all afternoon.

Surprise flittered over Brigg's features, and then his eyes went hard. "There's no problem. I was just taking this lady and her son to safety."

Christian turned to her. "Is that true?"

She thrust out her chin defiantly. "No, it's not true. The weasel was trying to force me to go with him."

The muscle in Christian's jaw twitched. "Yeah, that's what I thought." He straightened to his full height, several inches taller than Briggs. "I don't know what your game is, but you need to leave this woman alone."

"This has nothing to do with you, man," Briggs said.

Briggs had looked so threatening to Everly before. But compared to Christian, he was an overgrown frat boy, who'd gone soft around the edges. She was so grateful to have Christian in her corner, she could almost forget he'd been such a jerk earlier.

A perplexed look came over Briggs. "Hey you're Christian Ross." His eyes rounded to saucers, as he held up his hands. "Hey, I don't want no trouble."

"There won't be any trouble. All you have to do is turn around and walk away." Christian clenched his fists. "Your decision."

Briggs thrust out his chest. "Just because you're a hotshot celebrity doesn't give you the right to interfere in my business. You don't know who you're dealing with," he muttered, but Everly detected a slight stammer in his voice.

A hard amusement glittered in Christian's eyes. "Maybe you should enlighten me."

"You sure you wanna do this, Everly?" Briggs taunted.

"I told you to butt out of my business, but you wouldn't listen! You have no right to force me to go with you. And, you need to stop stalking me!" Anxiety was building to frenzy. She placed a hand on Christian's arm. "We need to get to safety."

He nodded. "Let's go."

Briggs shook his head. "Not gonna happen. I can't let her leave."

Christian chuckled. "You don't have much of a choice."

Briggs attempted to shove Christian backwards, but it was like trying to move a brick wall. Shock registered on Brigg's features, and he drew back a fist to strike. In a flash, Christian twisted him around, pinning his arm behind his back. Briggs doubled over and yelped in pain. Christian pushed him hard, sending Briggs sprawling, face-first in the dirt.

Briggs got up and backed away, a venomous expression on his beet-red face. "You've gone too far this time, Everly. I don't know how you got connected with this pretty boy, here, but Roland's not gonna like it. You know what, Ross? Your movies suck, almost as much as you do." He hurried off before Christian could react.

For some crazy reason, the scene struck Everly as funny. Here they were, on the side of a rural stretch of road, a steady stream of cars crawling by, while Roland's tough guy skulked off like a yellow-belly coward, hurling insults about a movie. All the while, a tsunami was bearing down on them. Everly had the feeling she'd left reality the moment she stepped foot on Hawaiian soil. She stifled her laugh, keeping a deadpan expression. "Well, I wouldn't say your movies suck ... exactly." Everly shrugged nonchalantly. "I mean, for action movies, they're not half bad."

Christian's eyes widened and he burst out laughing. "You're good."

She wasn't prepared for the dart of warmth that shot through her as their eyes met, sharing the moment.

Christian cocked his head. "By the way, who's Roland?"

She merely shook her head, as she plummeted back to reality.

"Mommy?"

Everly looked at Jordan, whose face was as white as his tennis shoes. In all the commotion, it hadn't occurred to her, he'd feel threatened by the violence. "We're going to the mountain. Can you walk?"

He shook his head *no*.

Weary and resigned, she bent down to pick him up.

"Here, let me." Christian leaned down so he was eye level with Jordan. "Hey, bud. Would you like to come to my house and play in the swimming pool with Sadie?"

Jordan nodded.

"Okay, let's go." Christian picked him up, placing him on his shoulders. Everly was surprised Jordan didn't protest.

Christian motioned with his head. "We need to get moving. According to the warning center, the first wave's expected to hit in less than an hour."

A sense of horror filled Everly. She didn't know how far up they needed to go, only that they needed to get as high above the ocean as they could. Her plan had been to simply follow the crowd to safety. When Christian started walking in another direction, she arched an eyebrow. "Where're we going?"

"To see Sadie, remember?"

Jordan giggled. "Silly mommy forgot already."

Christian smiled. "See, he knows what's going on. Smart boy."

Jordan beamed.

When Everly remained skeptical, he searched her eyes. "Do you trust me?"

Could she trust him? Even as the question entered her mind, warmth flowed through her. It was no coincidence that he showed up when he did. She knew as surely as she was standing here that he was the answer to her earlier prayer. "Yes."

He nodded. "Good."

They walked a few steps in silence before she spoke. "Thank you, for saving me from that creep."

"I figured it was the least I could do ... considering what happened earlier on the beach. I'm sorry I overreacted."

She shrugged. "It's okay."

"Truce?" He flashed a crooked grin that sent a parade of butterflies fluttering through her stomach, despite her best effort to be unaffected by his dashing, good looks.

"Truce."

A few minutes later, a thought occurred to her. "How did you happen to be on the side of the road, right where we were?"

He hesitated long enough for her to wonder if he was going to answer, but finally he spoke. "There's one main evacuation route from Sunset Beach to the mountains. I was hoping you would take it."

It took a second for her to process what he was saying. "Wait a minute? You came looking for me?"

He winced. "Yeah, I hope that doesn't sound too forward ... or weird. Like I said, I felt bad about the way things ended between us. And I figured you might need a hand with Jordan here." He squeezed Jordan's calf.

He'd come looking for her ... them. The notion was immensely pleasing.

"Of course, I didn't expect to find that lolo trying to attack you."

"Lolo?"

"Idiot. Sorry, that's my pidgin, or local talk, coming out."

"No need to apologize. I find it charming."

He chuckled. "Fo' real?"

She laughed. "Fo' real. See, it's not so hard to understand. This Southern Girl wasn't born yesterday."

He gave her a quirky look. "K'den, ono wahine, let's go to my hana to talk story or get grinds, wiki wiki."

"What?"

"You didn't understand?"

She made a face. "That was a cheap shot. Care to interpret?"

"I said, "Okay, great woman, let's go to my house to talk and get food ... pronto.""

She laughed. "Wow. I didn't get a word of that. And I've never been called great woman before."

He gave her an appraising look. "I just call it like I see it."

Warmth seeped into her cheeks. Incredible looks and charm. A lethal combination. She needed to keep her feet planted firmly on the ground. This was certainly not the time to throw caution to the wind and get swept off her feet by a savvy movie star who lived five thousand miles away. She needed to be practical about this. And the tsunami threat. She paused, the scope of their situation hitting her full force. "What do you think will happen if the tsunami's as big as the ones that hit Thailand or Japan?"

"Let's pray that doesn't happen. If it makes you feel any better, there've only been around eighty tsunamis that have hit the Hawaiian Islands over the past hundreds of years, and the majority of them have been small."

"So what you're saying is Hawaii's due for a big one."

He chuckled dryly. "I guess that's one way to look at it. You could also argue the stats are in our favor. If you're looking at the glass half full, that is."

"Sorry, didn't mean to come across as a Debbie Downer. I've had such rotten luck lately, that my first reaction is to fear the worst."

"I hear ya."

The sincerity in his voice struck a chord with her. From what she read, he'd had more than his share of heartache. Something they had in common.

She tried to think of something to say to lighten the mood, but nothing came. "I guess only time will tell, right?"

He nodded.

It had been a long, torturous day. Everly's calves were burning from the climb, and she was feeling a little short of breath. She was grateful when Christian stopped in front of a tall, wooden gate and said, "Well, here we are." He punched in a code, and the doors swung open. They stepped through and walked about a quarter of a mile down a paved driveway.

Everly looked ahead and saw a large, bungalow-style house with dark wood siding and a wrap-around porch. It sat in the center of some of the most exquisite grounds she'd ever seen. Her gaze moved over the manicured green grass and clusters of bushes bursting with colorful flowers. Just behind the house, she caught a ribbon of blue from the ocean, glistening in the distance. "This is your place?" She should've expected as much. After all, he was a famous actor. But this place was beyond anything she could've imagined—the epitome of paradise.

"Yes," Christian said a touch of pride in his voice. "You can't see it from here, but the pool's in the back.

Her heart dropped when she heard the sound of rushing water. Without thinking, she clutched Christian's arm, a wild look in her eyes. "That's not the tsunami coming in ... is it?"

Christian chuckled. "Thankfully, no. There's a waterfall in the back."

She wrinkled her nose. "A waterfall? Behind your house?"

"It frames the back of the pool."

"Oh." An estate with a waterfall overlooking the ocean. It was hard to fathom what it must be like to live in such a perfect place. Then she realized she was still holding his arm. As casually as she could, she let go.

When they got closer to the house, Sadie came out the front door and bounded down the steps, a middle-aged Hawaiian woman following behind.

Christian removed Jordan from his shoulders, placing him on the ground.

Sadie's dark eyes shined with excitement as she clapped her hands. "Jordan," she squealed.

"Hi, Sadie," Jordan said in a grownup tone.

"Would you like to play dolls with me?" Sadie asked shyly.

Jordan's eyes went round as he grimaced.

"Maybe you could play with the Legos instead," Christian inserted.

Sadie shrugged. "Okay, come, and I'll show you the playroom."

The woman stepped up to them and spoke to Christian. "I'm glad you're back. I was getting worried."

"It's a madhouse out there. The traffic's so backed up that people are walking up the hill."

She shook her head. "I was afraid of that."

"I'm glad Jarin and the boys were able to come here right away. Are they getting settled in?"

"Yep, they're on the back deck ... watching the ocean and eatin' all da grinds in da hana."

Christian turned to Everly. "All the food in the house," he explained.

She nodded. She understood most of what the woman said through context.

"Everly this is Mele. Mele ... Everly," Christian said.

When Everly held out her hand, to shake, Mele leaned in and air-kissed her on both cheeks instead. "Aloha."

"Aloha," Everly murmured, a little taken back by the warmth of the greeting.

A sly grin curved Mele's lips. "Now I see why Christian rushed out to find you." She winked at Christian. "She's just as beautiful as you said."

Everly was surprised ... in a good way. She looked at Christian who coughed like his throat was trying to swallow his tongue.

Mele laughed, eyes sparkling with mischief as she shoved Christian's arm. "See, he's so taken with you that he can't speak."

The situation was so awkward that Everly wasn't sure how to respond. Christian looked like he wanted to crawl under the grass, and Mele was enjoying every second of it. Judging from the way Mele teased Christian, she wondered if they were related. "Are you Sadie's mom?" She searched her memory. What was his sister's name? "Kat?"

Mele scrunched her nose. "Nah, nah, I'm no relation to this ugly kane."

Christian rolled his eyes. "Technically, Mele looks after the house and cooks the meals, but you'd think from the way she barks orders that she's my mother."

"You wish, brah. First of all, I'm way too young to have a son as old as you. But if you were my son, I would've whipped you into shape already." She tried to ruffle his hair, but he dodged her reach.

"See what I mean," he said, flicking his wrist. "Aye, aye aye ... bossy."

But the look of affection in his eyes was touching. It was obvious that he and Mele were super close.

Mele waved an arm. "Come inside. We'll go out back and watch the wave come in."

"Any news on how large the wave's expected to be?" Christian said.

"Nah. I don't think they know anything." Worry clouded her features. "Hopefully, it's just a false alarm, like all of the others have been."

Christian nodded. "I hope so." He paused. "Something smells good."

Jarin's cooking a slab of ribs on the grill. Whatever happens ... at least we'll have plenty a ono grinds to eat."

"Ono means good," Christian explained.

Everly nodded, committing the word to memory. She wondered if she was going to need an interpreter's guide to converse with Mele.

Christian frowned. "I didn't think we had any ribs left in the freezer."

"We didn't," Mele explained. "Jarin stopped and picked up a truckload on his way here."

Everly was surprised. "He took the time to stop by the grocery store?"

Mele chuckled. "Yeah, the whole island might float away, but Jarin's gonna make sure he has his ribs."

Everly glanced at the stretch of ocean, a sense of foreboding coming over her. "Do you think we're high enough here to be out the danger zone?"

A smile slipped over Christian's lips. "No worries. You're safe."

Safe. The word floated over her, as tantalizing as the succulent scent of meat in the evening air. She'd been living in Roland's shadow for so long that she couldn't remember when she last felt safe. And yet, here, on this estate with Christian, anything seemed possible. Maybe it was wishful thinking ... but it was something to hold onto.

CHAPTER 6

Everly looked out over the back deck to the sky ablaze with orange and yellow swirls from the setting sun, reminding her of orange and pineapple sherbet. A slight breeze ruffled her hair. It seemed a perfect evening. Had she not heard the weather reports and the sirens going off every hour, Everly wouldn't have realized anything was amiss. Growing up in the South, she'd always feared tornadoes and had spent many a day, huddled in a basement, waiting for the storm to pass. But at least with a tornado, there were warning signs in the weather patterns. With a tsunami there was no warning, other than an unusually low tide. No wonder the people on the beach in Thailand didn't realize what was happening until the wave hit.

On the surface, it seemed like everyone was taking everything in stride, but Everly sensed an underlying nervousness to the group. Jarin was at the grill, and sons were playing games on their phones. But they all kept glancing towards the ocean. Mele buzzed back and forth from the kitchen to the deck, bringing out enough food to last a week. Everly got the feeling Mele was staying busy to keep her mind off the threat. Jordan and Sadie were building a Lego tower, the only two who were oblivious to what was going on.

Christian was sitting beside her, his long, brown, muscular legs casually crossed. Everly was hyper-aware of his presence. It was like an invisible string pulling them together. Of course, it didn't hurt that he was one of the best-looking men she'd ever seen, and he looked better in real life than he did on film. She was captivated by the sparkle in his light eyes and the dimple that appeared on his right cheek when he smiled. But it was more than his looks that drew her attention. There was kindness in his soulful eyes, but she could also sense sadness. Or maybe she just imagined that part because of what she knew about him. No, it was there ... she could feel it. It tugged at that part of her. He'd suffered as she had. On a practical note, she appreciated how protective he was with Sadie, keeping a watchful eye over her. He was jovial with Jarin and his sons, laughing and making jokes. He and Mele teased one another relentlessly, like brother and sister.

Everly came to Hawaii ... hoping to get a reprieve from Roland and to find answers about Mitchell. It was crazy to think she'd ended up here, with Christian Ross, one of the most famous actors of the day, and yet she felt perfectly at ease. Well, she would've felt perfectly at ease, were it not for the tsunami threat.

Jarin pointed. "You'd better finish off that plate, Everly, because I've got another slab with your name written all over it."

Everly's eyes widened as she looked down at her half-eaten plate of food. Her stomach was stretched to the point of exploding. Accustomed to large, Southern meals, she'd never seen anyone put away as much food as Jarin and his sons. Not wanting to be rude, she'd eaten as much as she could. But the minute she cleaned her plate, Jarin piled on another helping.

Casually, Christian draped an arm around her chair. A spark of electricity pulsed through her when he leaned in and whispered in her ear, his warm breath tickling her skin. "You'd better keep eating, or Jarin might get his feelings hurt."

Her face fell. "This is my fourth plate," she whispered. "I can't eat another bite." Then she saw Jarin watching her closely and realized he and Christian were in cahoots. She eyed them, her eyes sparking. "How many plates were you gonna give me?"

Jarin laughed. "As many as you'd eat."

A devilish smile curved Christian's lips. "Jarin bet you'd eat two plates ... I said three."

"And she showed you guys up," Mele piped in. "Good for you, Everly. I knew I liked you."

Everly shoved Christian's arm, a mock scowl forming over her face. "That was mean."

He grinned sheepishly. "Sorry ... I couldn't resist."

"Uh, huh. I see how it is." She pushed aside the plate, pointing a finger at Christian. "I'll blame you when I can't fit into any of my jeans."

"I guess that means we'll have to work out tomorrow ... burn off the extra calories."

"Tomorrow ... huh? And what makes you so sure I'll be here tomorrow?" she quipped.

Christian touched her arm, sincerity shining in his eyes. "I wish you would stay."

Heat bubbled over her as her mind grappled with what was happening. Out of nowhere, the atmosphere had shifted to something intensely personal. Blood started pumping like a freight train through her veins. Things were moving fast ... maybe too fast. A look passed between Mele and Jarin, and they suddenly grew interested in their mundane tasks, turning away to give them privacy.

Christian's eyes locked with hers. "Please ... stay a few days. I've got plenty of room."

There were a million reasons why she shouldn't ... Roland being at the top of the list. The minute Briggs told him about Christian, he'd go berserk and make things very difficult for her. "But tomorrow's Christmas Eve."

His eyes flickered with what looked like pain. "I know."

His reaction was a bit confusing at first, and then she recalled. His former girlfriend committed suicide on Christmas Eve. Should she stay? She weighed it in her mind. Christmas alone with Jordan in a small beach rental, or Christmas here in this luxurious place ... with

Christian and Sadie. "Okay," she said, almost before her mind could process what she was saying.

"Good," he said, breathing what looked to be a sigh of relief. "Thank you," he said sincerely. When his striking eyes captured hers, everything around them seemed to disappear. The moment got deliciously slow. She glanced at his lips, wondering what it would be like to kiss him.

When Jarin cleared his throat, she backed away from Christian, blushing. But Christian didn't seem one bit embarrassed. On the contrary, his eyes were brimming with what could only be described as a cautious hope. She gave him a questioning look, wishing she could read his mind.

"Look!" Jarin's oldest son pointed to the ocean. They all looked toward it and saw the large wave rolling in.

Everly held her breath, praying it would stop at the shoreline. Thankfully it did.

Mele was the first to speak. "Was that the tsunami?"

Jarin peered out. "Maybe. The tide looks higher than it was a while ago."

Mele frowned. "You think? It's hard to tell from this distance. All da waves look high to me."

"That's a good sign, yes?" Jarin said.

Christian hurried inside to check the news. When he returned a few minutes later, his expression was one of relief. "The tsunami warning has been lifted."

"Thank the Lord," Mele said, hugging Jarin.

Everly was surprised when Christian encircled her in a tight hug. His breath smelled like the tangy salsa and chips he'd been eating, and she felt the strength of his embrace. For a split second, she had a feeling of déjà vu ... like coming home to something familiar. Before she could analyze the feeling, it fled, leaving her to wonder if she'd only imagined it. She noticed he held onto her a few minutes longer than necessary.

When Christian let her go, Everly said a silent prayer of thankfulness that she and Jordan were safe. She knew they'd been watched over today. Now that the threat was over, she suddenly felt exhausted from the day's events. What she would give for a soft bed and a few hours of sleep. She stifled a yawn.

Christian quickly picked up on her thoughts. "You look tired."

"Yeah, it's been a long day. Would it be too much to ask you to take Jordan and me back to the beach rental?"

A crease appeared between his brows. "I thought we'd settled this already. You're staying here."

"Oh, I just assumed since the tsunami is over that we'd go back there to sleep. You've been so kind to us already. I don't want to be a burden."

"You're not," he replied firmly.

Part of her really did want to stay here with Christian, but she didn't want to make things any sticker with Roland than they already were. Besides, she and Christian lived worlds apart. There was no future for them. "We can still come for Christmas."

Mele shook her head. "With all the traffic, it'll take several hours to get back down the hill. Your best bet is to stay here for the night. That's what my family's gonna do. We're staying in the cottage. You and Jordan can take one of the guest rooms in the main house."

"Please, Mommy," Jordan piped in. "Can we stay?"

There was a hopeful expression on Christian's handsome face, but he wasn't putting undue pressure on her, like Roland would have. Rather, he seemed willing to wait for her to make her own decision. "What about the rental car? I have all of my luggage in it."

"No worries. I'll take you to get the car in the morning," Christian said. "Things should be back to normal by then."

She could tell that no matter what objection she put forth, either Christian or Mele would fire back a solution. She sighed. "All right, we'll stay." She turned to Christian. "Thanks so much."

He nodded. "Of course."

Her phone buzzed. She pulled it out ... Roland. Her stomach tightened. Briggs probably spoke to him by now. If she didn't answer, he would keep calling. "Excuse me for a minute. I need to take this."

Christian leaned back in the lounge chair and stretched out his legs, letting the darkness of the night envelope him as he listened to the hypnotic sound of the waterfall, spilling over the rocks. After he'd gotten Everly and Jordan settled into their room, he got Sadie ready for bed. It had taken a full hour and several bedtime stories to lull Sadie to sleep, due to her excitement about Jordan sleeping over and Christmas Eve tomorrow.

His thoughts went to Everly and all that took place during the course of the day. From the moment he met her, she'd consumed his thoughts. First, due to the instant attraction he felt toward her and second, because he regretted arguing with her. When he learned about the tsunami threat, all he could think about was getting Everly and Jordan to safety. It baffled him to feel such a strong connection with a woman he'd just met.

It was a miracle he'd found Everly in the midst of the commotion. He'd been driving down Pupukea Road, making pretty good time going against traffic, when he spotted Everly, struggling with that man, Briggs. So, he'd parked his SUV alongside the road and gone to her aid. At first, he assumed Briggs was a stranger. But then he realized with a jolt that Everly knew him. And then there was the mysterious Roland. Briggs mentioned that name when threatening Everly. When Christian asked Everly who Roland was, she clammed up. The same name came up on Everly's phone when she received the call. Even though Everly stepped to the edge of the deck, Christian could tell from the tone of her voice she'd gotten into a heated argument with the person on the phone. It troubled Christian that Everly accused Briggs of stalking her. Had Briggs followed her here? It certainly sounded that way.

Instinct told Christian Everly was attracted to him too, and when she said she wasn't married, he assumed that meant she was available. But maybe he'd jumped the gun. Roland obviously had some sort of hold over Everly. Were the two romantically involved? The jealousy that stabbed through him came as a surprise. He thought again how crazy it was that he could be so affected by a woman he'd just met. But, he couldn't deny the charge that went through him when he held her in his arms immediately after the tsunami.

It had been touch-and-go for a few minutes there, but he was glad he'd persuaded Everly to spend the night. For weeks, he'd been dreading Christmas Eve like the plague. But now, it didn't seem as daunting, with Everly and Jordan here. His parents were returning from their cruise late tomorrow evening and planned on coming for Christmas. Kat was flying back Christmas morning and would be joining them later on in the day.

Christian smiled thinking about how animated Everly's hazel eyes had become and the heightened color in her face when she realized he was teasing her about the food. And, the hungry look in her eyes that kindled those same feelings in him, especially when he realized she wanted him to kiss her. Or maybe it was wishful thinking on his part, but that's the vibe he got. At any rate, he certainly wanted to kiss her. He glanced toward the house and the soft halo of light that came from the guest room. Even the house seemed more cheerful with her here. Nighttime often left him feeling despondent and lonely, especially this time of the year. But tonight, anticipation tingled through him. He wondered if Everly had purchased presents for Jordan. If she hadn't, he would need to make a trip into Mililani to Costco or Super Walmart. He'd never shopped for a boy before. It would be fun to be able to get something other than Barbie dolls or bake sets.

A slight rustle from behind caught his attention, and he sat up, his senses on full alert. He cocked his ears, listening. This time, he heard the slight crack of a stick breaking. His muscles grew taut as he stood and turned around. "Who's there?"

Nothing.

He strained to hear. Was someone there? Watching? Chills ran down his spine.

He stood there for a full five minutes, his eyes scoping the dark landscape. For months, Mele had been after him to get motion sensors for the grounds. Especially since they got reporters nosing around from time to time. But Christian had resisted the idea. He felt equipped to deal with most situations. Growing up in Laie had made him tougher than most to start with. But when he reached stardom, he figured he had two options—live in the shadow of body guards 24/7 or learn the art of combat. He'd chosen the latter, hiring a former Navy Seal to teach him how to handle himself. Not only had the training given him peace of mind, it allowed him to do his own stunts. Even so, at this moment he felt vulnerable and wondered if he should've taken Mele's advice. After all, no amount of combat training could protect him against a gun. "Show yourself," he demanded, clenching his fists.

The only response was the slight ruffling of his hair when the breeze picked up. Finally, he turned and began walking towards the house.

When Roland's phone buzzed, he carefully got out of bed, so as not to awake the sleeping blonde beside him. He padded across the carpet of his luxury condo to the solid wall of windows that afforded a spectacular view of the water. "Hey."

"I'm here at the estate," Briggs said quietly. "It looks like Everly and Jordan are staying the night. Ross just stepped back into the house."

Roland swore under his breath.

"What do you want me to do?"

He clenched his jaw and balled his fist, resting it on the window. "Keep watching them. I want a full report."

"Will do."

Roland ended the call, fury burning through him like poison. The thoughts of Everly being alone with Christian Ross was almost more than he could take. He'd been on pins and needles from the moment he realized Everly was in Hawaii. It infuriated him that she would leave town without telling him. And when he learned about the tsunami warning, he panicked and instructed Briggs to get Everly and Jordan to safety. But that had blown up in his face, resulting in

Everly taking up with—of all people—Christian Ross. Talk about rotten luck. Roland was accustomed to circulating in the upper realm of society and there were few people he considered to be out of his league. But Christian Ross? Billionaire Movie Star? Geez! How was he supposed to compete with that? He couldn't even fathom how Everly could've met the man, much less formed an attachment to him.

Why couldn't Everly understand that he loved her? Hadn't he proved his love when he looked after her and Jordan following Mitchell's disappearance? Yeah, there'd been other women, but they were insignificant ... mere distractions. He was a virile man, after all, with needs that had to be met. But his heart belonged to Everly. It always had and it always would.

The first time he walked into Global Fitness Center in Charleston and saw Everly, he knew she was destined to be his. She was teaching a Pilates class. Her eyes met his for one brief moment, and he had the feeling he was truly seeing the sun for the first time. After that, he was a changed man and could think of nothing except how to win her heart. Then he got to know her and learned she'd recently gotten married. But he wasn't about to let a little thing like that stand in his way. He'd fought his way to the top of his law class at Yale, graduating with the highest honors. Then, he built his law firm from the ground up with sheer guts and determination. It didn't take long for him to ingratiate himself into Mitchell's life. Mitchell was vain and self-indulgent, intent on making a name for himself in society. All Roland had to do was dangle the bait of investing in Mitchell's art gallery, and before long, the two were as thick as thieves. Of course, it never entered Mitchell's mind that Roland was using him to get to Everly. Mitchell was too self-centered to see anything but himself, a character flaw Roland exploited to the fullest extent.

When Everly became pregnant with Jordan, Mitchell resented her for it. And when the two started having marital problems, Roland decided it was the perfect time to make his move. He began by planting seeds in Mitchell's mind, painting him a picture of all that he was sacrificing being married, instead of single. Then he invited him to glitzy parties with glamorous women who, for a pittance, would tell a man anything he wanted to hear. The plan unfolded like a well-orchestrated play as the wedge between Mitchell and Everly grew larger. Then Roland used his influence with local law enforcement to turn up the heat, putting Mitchell under investigation for fraudulent business dealings. The best part was Mitchell never knew Roland was the instigator of the investigation. As far as Mitchell was concerned, Roland was his closest friend and confidant. And then came the finale—he gave Mitchell a large amount of money, helped him fake his death and disappear.

Briggs thought it absurd that Roland went to all that trouble to help Mitchell disappear when he could've, just as easily, put a bullet in his head and dumped him in the lake. But Briggs was a machine, acting without sentiment or feeling, whereas, Roland was more genteel and refined. In fact, Roland had developed a surprising fondness for Mitchell and wished him well, so long as he stayed out of Everly's life.

Marriage to Everly was a dream come true, until she grew jealous and started snooping into his private affairs. If only she'd kept her nose out of his business, the two of them would still be happily married. He'd given her every comfort and treated Jordan like his own child, which was not an easy task, considering Jordan was the spitting image of Mitchell. When Everly demanded a divorce he reluctantly agreed, but only because he knew he could maintain control over her. There had been plenty of suitors who set their caps at Everly over the past two and a half years, but he systematically took care of them. He figured it was only a matter of time before Everly came back to him. What he hadn't counted on, however, was her escaping to Hawaii and meeting a famous actor. Blood throbbed in his temples. There was no way he was gonna give Everly up. She belonged to him. One way or another Christian Ross was going to have to recognize that. He forced himself to look at the situation analytically. The next logical steps were to find out all he could about Ross, discover his weaknesses, and exploit them. If that didn't work, he'd be forced to get rid of him.

"Hey, where'd you go? Come back to bed," the blonde purred.

"In a minute," he said, not bothering to hide the annoyance in his voice. An image of Everly flashed before his eyes—her heart-shaped face, stubborn chin, lively eyes, and lush, curly hair. And the best thing about Everly—she was opinionated, not some simple-headed puppet who'd tell him anything he wanted to hear. Her sauciness enthralled him. And she was smart. He could almost see the outline of her delicate shoulders, tapering to a small waist and shapely legs. Her light floral perfume invaded his senses, and he longed for her to the point where it hurt.

The woman came up behind him and started rubbing his shoulders. He'd picked her up at a bar the night before, couldn't even remember her name. She encircled his waist and snuggled close to him. "Come to bed. I'm lonely without you."

Roland turned to face her, hardly seeing her beauty in front of him. All he could think about was Everly. Suddenly, it angered him that this woman was here instead of her. When she reached up to caress his face, he slapped her hand away.

Smudges of scarlet stained her cheeks as a petulant frown formed on her face. "What was that for?"

He pushed her away, feeling dead and empty inside. "You need to leave."

"Hey, baby. Don't be like this. I know just what you need," she said softly.

"Get out!"

Her eyes lassoed. "What?"

"You heard me." He turned his back to her and stared unseeingly at the dark night.

The woman let out a long string of curse words, which he barely heard. Then she grabbed her things and left in a huff, slamming the door behind her.

Roland placed a hand against the cold glass. "Come back to me, Everly," he uttered. "For both of our sakes ... please come back."

CHAPTER 7

It was one of those perfect, blue-sky evenings for which California was known, a salty breeze floating up along the Pacific Coast Highway. Everything was right in the world. Christian's latest movie had broken box office records its opening weekend, and negotiations were underway for a third movie in the Jase Scott action series. All of his hard work was starting to pay off, and to celebrate, Christian had bought a new sports car. He gripped the steering wheel, appreciating how his sleek red Ferrari 458 Convertible Spider hugged the road, almost anticipating the turns before he made them. Growing up poor, he never could've imagined he would be living such a charmed life.

"Faster," Heather urged, her long hair whipping in her face.

He pressed his foot on the accelerator, and the power was instant, catapulting them forward at a light-speed pace.

"Whoo!" Heather lifted her hands in the air. Also an actress, Christian and Heather first met when they co-starred in his first movie. At the time, she was more well-known than he. He'd asked her out at least a dozen times before she agreed to go on a date with him. They'd dated on and off for several years but were now seeing each other exclusively.

The scene changed, Heather was driving. "This is the life," she exclaimed, sheer exhilaration sounding in her voice. One of the things Christian most appreciated about Heather was her gift for living in the moment—blissfully happy and completely alive. His parents didn't much care for Heather, probably for that same reason and because they saw her as a social climber, who only wanted to date him because of his superstar status. Deep down, he suspected that was probably the case, but life with Heather was fun and thrilling. She knew all the right people and they went to all the right parties. And at the moment, Christian had no desire to settle down.

"Let's see what this baby can do," Heather said, speeding up.

They rounded a couple of curves, and Christian could feel the car nearly slipping out of Heather's control. They were going fast ... too fast! Heather was a daredevil, always pushing the envelope. "Hey, slow down," he cautioned.

Heather laughed. "Party pooper," she drawled, pursing her Botoxed lips and blowing him a kiss.

Christian relaxed a fraction when they came up behind a slow-moving van. Now Heather would be forced to slow down. But she jerked the wheel to pass and had to pull back when she realized a semi-truck was coming in the other direction.

"What're you doing?" Christian demanded. "Just stay behind the van."

"I'm the one driving," she sniffed, leaning her head out to see around the van. "Coast is clear," she chimed, swerving into the oncoming traffic.

Christian's heart lurched when he saw the car, a short distance ahead, coming right towards them. "Step on it," he yelled.

"I can make it." Heather pressed on the gas. As she got even with the van, it sped up. She put the pedal to the floor, trying to get ahead. By the time she passed it, the approaching car was almost upon them. She swerved to get over in her lane, but the back of the Ferrari clipped the front of the van.

Everything seemed to slow down, Christian sensed it all in excruciating detail. The horror on Heather's face as the car spun out of control. The helpless feeling as he bounced around uncontrollably.

The sound of metal crunching. The pain that ripped through his body. The acrid smoke filling his lungs.

He cried out, and then he was falling.

Everly sat up in bed, darkness pressing against her eye sockets. It took a second for her eyes to adjust so she could see. For a split second, she was disoriented, before remembering she was at Christian's home. She'd been having that same wretched dream about Mitchell, diving at Lake Tahoe. Except this time, as Mitchell's body sank and she went after him, his face transformed into Roland. Before she could pull away, he clutched her hand in an iron grip, dragging her down into the cold, murky water. She shuddered, grateful it was only a dream.

What had awoken her? Jordan? No, he was sleeping soundly beside her. She looked at the pale moonlight seeping through the edges of the curtains as she reached for her phone—2:45 a.m. She lay back against the pillow and was drifting back to sleep when she heard the noise. She stilled, listening. It sounded like a muffled cry. She waited. There it was again. She got out of bed and slipped on her shorts and t-shirt from the day before. Unfortunately, that was all she had to wear until she could get her luggage.

She knew Christian's room was right next to hers. He'd pointed that out in case she needed something during the night. She stepped into the hall. The house was eerily quiet, making her wonder if she'd only imagined the sound. There was something unnerving about being the only person awake in an unfamiliar house. And even though she'd felt an instant connection with Christian, he was a virtual stranger. A shiver ran down her spine as she hugged her arms. Spending the night here felt so logical earlier, but now, in the dead of the night, she questioned her judgment. Christian's door was partially open. She cocked her ears, listening. Had she just imagined the noise? She was about to go back to bed, then heard it again. This time, it was an unmistakable cry, coming from Christian's room. She stole towards the door and peeked in.

"Christian?" she said softly. "Are you okay?"

He didn't answer. She peered through the darkness and could make out his sleeping form in the bed.

She heard a gurgle, followed by soft moans. Her feet acted before she had time to think and strode across the room to his bed. She stood beside him and realized instantly what was happening. He was having a nightmare, his face twisting in pain. She touched his arm, and he jerked, opening his eyes. But she could tell he was still half asleep as he looked right through her.

Suddenly, she felt foolish for charging into his bedroom and waking him up. "Are you okay?"

He shook his head as if coming out of a daze. His eyes came into focus as he sat up in bed and leaned back against the pillow. Then he seemed to realize she was there. "Everly," he said, sleep coating his voice. "Is everything okay?" He reached and flicked on the lamp. It was then Everly noticed he was bathed in sweat. He rubbed his hands through his hair, pulling a single curl into the center of his forehead.

How was it possible for a man to look so adorable and sexy at the same time? And then Everly realized he was shirtless. Her throat turned to sandpaper as she swallowed. He was like a moving sculpture with his chiseled pecs and abs. She forced her eyes to his face as an explanation tumbled out. "I heard something, and I wasn't sure what it was. It woke me up. So, I came to see what the noise was. And your door was open. I'm very sorry I intruded. Goodnight."

She turned, intending to scamper away as quickly as possible before she made a complete idiot of herself.

"Hey."

"Yeah?"

"Would you like to have a cup of hot chocolate with me?" When she didn't answer, a wry grin formed over his lips. "Please?"

"Sure."

"Give me a minute to get dressed, and I'll meet you in the kitchen."

"Okay."

––––––––

Everly took a sip of hot chocolate. "Umm ... very good. I'm impressed."

Christian joined her at the table. "Thanks."

"What's your secret?"

He flashed a mischievous grin. "A guy can't give away all his secrets."

She laughed. "Oh, I see how it is." She took another sip. "That's okay. I bet I can figure it out."

"Really? This, I've gotta see."

"There's cinnamon in it."

"Yep. But that's pretty obvious."

"It kind of has an egg nog flavor. Is it a creamer?"

He sat back in his chair. "Nope."

"Okay, you've got me. I have no idea."

"Turmeric."

She wrinkled her nose. "Turmeric? Like the spice?"

"Yep."

"The stuff they put in curry?"

"Yes."

"Hmm ... I never would've guessed that."

Christian's gaze flickered over her. She raked a self-conscious hand through her hair. She could only imagine how awful she must look. Not a speck of makeup, and her hair was all over the place, even curlier than usual due to the humidity.

"You look great," he said, as if reading her mind.

She rolled her eyes. "Yeah ... right."

"I'm serious."

"Thank you." His eyes met hers, and she was struck by how green they were. She couldn't help but voice the question that had been on her mind since she'd met Christian. "Your eyes ... they're an unusual color for a Polynesian."

"My mom's Tongan and my dad's Haole."

"Haole?"

"White. The term *Haole* actually means foreigner, but most locals use it to refer to Caucasians."

That explained it. His features looked more Caucasian, and he was slighter and thinner than most Polynesians she'd seen. "Did you grow up here?"

"Yes, in a little town called Laie, only a few miles up the road."

"Where the Polynesian Cultural Center's located."

He was impressed.

"I was going to take Jordan there last night," she explained. "He wanted to see the fire-knife dancers."

He winced. "I'm sorry your evening got wrecked. This is probably not turning out to be the greatest vacation, huh?"

She tucked a loose curl behind her ear. "Well, it's definitely different from what I expected."

His eyes held hers. "Different can be good."

The pull to him was so strong that she gripped her cup in order to keep from reaching out and touching him. A small smile touched her lips. "Absolutely." She was itching to ask him about the nightmare and kept hoping he would bring it up. His demeanor was so calm and relaxed that had she not seen his anguish firsthand, she wouldn't have believed it. Silence settled between them, and she sought for something to say. She glanced around the airy kitchen with neutral tones, gleaming countertops, and streamlined cabinets. It was distinctly masculine with the strong, clean lines. "I love the dark wood. What kind is it?"

"Koa. It grows here on the islands."

"It's really beautiful."

He leaned back in his chair and took a drink from his mug, studying her. "So, Everly, I want to know all about you. What do you like to do? Besides exercise?"

She thought for a minute. Did she have any outside interests? Her life revolved around Jordan and work. That didn't leave much time for anything else. "I like to cook," she finally said.

"Well, I like to eat, so there you go. See, we have lots in common."

She laughed. "Spoken like a true man."

"Tell me something else about you."

"I like to read."

"What types of books?"

"Romantic suspense. I'm a sucker for Mary Higgins Clark."

He made a face. "I think we're gonna have to agree to disagree there."

"You don't like to read?"

"No, I've never been much of a reader."

She was surprised and a little disappointed. As far as she was concerned a voracious reader equaled an intelligent person. Her thoughts must've shown on her face because he laughed. "Don't look at me like that."

"Like what?"

"Like ... I'm a moron."

Her face flamed. "I wasn't thinking that."

"Yes, you were." An irresistible grin curved his lips, highlighting his dimple.

"How can you not like to read?"

He shrugged. "I guess I was always too busy playing sports and surfing. Don't get me wrong, I read a lot of articles ... abstracts ... that sort of thing. I just don't enjoy reading fiction."

She gave him a pointed look. "Well, what do you enjoy doing?"

"Acting."

She wagged a finger. "Something other than your profession."

"Gardening."

"Really?" She wouldn't have pegged him as a gardener. But then again, the grounds of the estate were immaculate.

"Gardening helps me relax. I also enjoy painting."

"That's impressive. I took a watercolor class once."

"How was it?"

She grimaced. "Dreadful."

He laughed. "It couldn't have been all that bad."

"Trust me. It was. The teacher was tickled pink when I didn't sign up for her next class."

Time seemed to fly as they sat, chatting about inconsequential things. When Everly drank the last sip of her hot chocolate, she yawned. "I'd better get back to bed." She was about to stand, but he placed a hand over hers.

"Tell me about Roland," he implored.

The comment was a bucket of ice water that jarred her back to reality. Roland had been belligerent on the phone, accusing her of all sorts of ridiculous things. He even had the gall to suggest that she'd planned the entire trip to Hawaii, just so she could hook up with Christian. He wouldn't listen to reason, so she finally had to hang up on him. He was insanely jealous, to the point where she was becoming afraid of him. She looked across the table at Christian. It had been fun to pretend for a moment that she could live in Christian's world, feel his protective arms around her, and know that everything would be okay. But it was only a dream—a dream that would end all too quickly the minute she stepped foot on the mainland.

He rubbed his thumb across the top of her hand. "Please. Tell me."

Energy surged through her, and she couldn't help but appreciate how his skin felt on hers. She eyed him. "Okay. But only if you'll tell me about your nightmare." A muscle twitched in his jaw, and she thought for a second he might refuse. But finally, he nodded.

"Roland's my ex-husband."

He nodded. "I figured as much." Wariness seeped into his eyes. "Are you still involved with him?"

She belted out a harsh laugh. "Not hardly!"

Christian looked relieved.

"Well, let me rephrase that. My involvement with Roland starts and stops with Jordan."

"Well, yeah, as his father it's only natural that he would have a say about Jordan."

She was trying to decide how much of her sordid past she wanted to divulge, but her thoughts must've been written all over her face because Christian cocked his head. "There's more to the story, isn't there?"

She tilted her head. "How do you do that?"

"What?"

"Pick up on my thoughts like that. Are you always so intuitive?"

"Only with people I care about."

His voice was a caress that sent a tingle running down her spine. "But we've only just met."

"Time is irrelevant when it comes to matters of the heart," he said softly.

The passionate look in his eye evoked a longing she could scarcely contain. Her eyes traced the strong curve of his jaw and the light stubble across it. For so long, she'd told herself that she didn't need another man in her life. After all, she was independent and at the top of her game, career-wise, so that if she played her cards right, she would own a fitness center within the next five years. Furthermore, she had a beautiful little boy that she loved with all of her heart. But being here with Christian made her realize that she did want someone—a companion with which to share life's joys and heartaches.

"So, tell me the rest of your story."

The tenderness in his voice was a healing balm. And she found herself opening up in a way she rarely did. She told him the whole story, starting with Roland. Their marriage. How he'd adopted Jordan. Then she told about his multiple affairs with other women. She even told Christian about Mitchell and how she'd come here, partly because she wanted to know if he was still alive. When she finished, she sat back in her seat, feeling drained but relieved that she'd gotten it off her chest. A part of her wondered if Christian would turn and run, now that he knew.

Christian drummed his fingers on the table. "So, you've had no contact with the detective since he called you the one time?"

"No, I've tried to call several times but his number has been disconnected."

He looked thoughtful. "Have you gone to the police?"

"That's my next step. I didn't want to start asking too many questions before I came here, because if Mitchell really did fake his death, then there's a chance he'll run." She sighed. "The whole thing seems absurd. I just can't believe Mitchell would fake his own death. But the crux of it is ... he left one day for a diving trip and never came home. And there was never a body."

"What happens if he's alive?"

The tone of Christian's voice was light, but she could tell from the conflicted look in his eyes that he was asking if she still had feelings for Mitchell.

"Things between us were already rocky before Mitchell died ... err ... disappeared. Any feelings I had for him died a long time ago, but it would be nice to have closure. You know what I mean?"

His eyes turned to fathomless pools of deep emerald as he nodded.

She reached for his hand. "Tell me about the nightmare. Judging by how quickly you rebounded from it, I'm assuming it happens quite often."

"Yes," he admitted, "although it gets worse this time of the year."

She remained quiet, sensing he needed space in which to voice his thoughts.

"All of my life, I wanted to become an actor. In the beginning, my parents indulged me. They allowed me to take a few acting lessons, that sort of thing. But deep down, they assumed I'd eventually grow out of the idea." He chuckled. "They about flipped their lids when I told them I was moving to L.A. to pursue acting full time."

"I'll bet." She gave him an admiring look. "But you did it."

He sighed. "Yes, I beat the odds and became an actor."

"Not just any actor, but a superstar."

"Yeah. When I landed the lead role in the Jase Scott series, I thought I'd hit the jackpot. I assumed all my troubles would be over." He chuckled ruefully. "Of course, I had no way of knowing what was ahead." His eyes took on a distant look. "When *Freefall* and *Lethal Target* did so well, I reached stardom overnight. When *Crossfire* was released things got even crazier. Everybody wanted a piece of Christian Ross. The irony is, I started to lose touch with who I really was. The star took over, and before long, I didn't even recognize myself. Then, the accident happened." He reached for his empty mug, absently turning it over in his hands. "I shouldn't have let Heather drive that day. The thing is … I knew it was a bad idea, but she kept after me, so I caved." His brows knitted together, a tortured look coming over him. "One stupid decision affects everything."

She nodded in understanding. She couldn't count the number of times she'd thought—*If only I'd asked Mitchell to stay home and not go on his diving trip.*

"The car was totaled. Miraculously, I came away with only a broken arm and a few cuts and bruises. But Heather …" his voice caught "… Heather was paralyzed from the waist down. Heather was one of those free spirits, who refused to be tied down. The last time I saw her, she told me that she couldn't spend the rest of her life in a wheelchair." His voice grew hoarse. "I just thought she was in denial. I had no idea she was planning to take her own life." He swallowed and looked away.

A tear slipped from the corner of Everly's eye and dribbled a crooked path down her cheek. Hastily, she wiped it away with the palm of her hand. Then she scooted her chair next to Christian. She placed a hand on his arm. "I'm sorry."

"After Heather died, I could no longer tolerate the Hollywood scene. So, I did the only thing I could think to do—I came home … here. This place helped put me back together." A grim smile touched his lips. "But unfortunately, it doesn't stop the nightmares. Today marks the third anniversary of Heather's death."

Her mouth rounded. "Oh, I didn't know that. I'm so sorry." No wonder Christian had been so adamant about her and Jordan spending Christmas with him. "Hey," she said firmly. "It wasn't your fault. You know that, right?"

He nodded, but she could see guilt simmering in his eyes. It was much easier to say it than to believe it yourself. Heck, she'd wasted a lot of time feeling guilty about things she couldn't control. Her pregnancy with Jordan was not something she planned. She'd always wanted children, but Mitchell wanted to wait a while. When it happened, she was thrilled and assumed Mitchell would feel the same way. But he started to resent her and the baby. So, she felt guilty for getting pregnant—even though she'd taken all the necessary precautions to prevent it. And then, when Mitchell disappeared, she felt guilty because she didn't ask him to stay home. Her guilt playing out in those stupid dreams of being in the water with him. And even though it was absurd, the tiniest part of her felt somewhat responsible for Roland's infidelity, like maybe if she'd been a better wife to him, he wouldn't have looked elsewhere. Guilt wasn't rational, no amount of levelheaded thinking erased it. The feelings were always there. The trick was seeing them for what they were and moving on. Sitting here, feeling Christian's pain, caused something to shift inside her. After her conversation with Roland, she'd almost convinced herself it'd be best for her and Jordan to leave Hawaii, first thing in the morning, just to get him off her back. But now, she saw things differently. Maybe it wasn't coincidental that she and Jordan were here during Christian's critical time. At the very least, they provided a distraction from the memories. "Hey, I was thinking that maybe tomorrow you and Sadie could show Jordan and me around the island."

He brightened. "Really?"

"Yeah, the only thing we've done thus far is go to the beach."

"It would be my pleasure." He rewarded her with a brilliant smile that melted her insides. "Oh, I meant to ask ... do you have plenty of presents for Jordan?"

"I packed as many as I could into a suitcase." She winced. "Hopefully, my luggage is okay." She didn't even want to contemplate what she would do if their clothes and Jordan's Christmas presents got stolen.

"I'm sure it's fine. We'll check on it first thing in the morning. If you need any last-minute gift items, we can get them tomorrow." He gave her a tender look. "Thank you."

"For what?"

"For listening."

"You're welcome," she said sincerely. Their eyes locked, and she had the impression he was seeing into her soul. Pretty surprising considering they'd known each other less than twenty-four hours. Nevertheless, she couldn't deny the strong connection they shared.

"You are so beautiful." He caressed the side of her face.

Her pulse quickened as a rush of anticipation swept through her. When he leaned in, she parted her lips expectantly. She'd been wanting to kiss him all day—to taste his lips against hers. Run her fingers through his dense mop of curly hair.

"Mommy."

She drew back in a hard snap that caused her to come to her senses. "Jordan. What're you doing up?"

Jordan rubbed his eyes. "I'm thirsty."

She stood. "Okay, let me get you a drink, and we'll go back to bed." She got Jordan situated and was about to leave the kitchen when Christian caught her hand, a look of promise in his eyes.

"See you tomorrow."

"Yes, see you then," she said, hurrying out, mostly because she wasn't sure how to act. On the one hand, she'd really wanted to kiss Christian. But it was probably for the best that Jordan interrupted them. After all, there was no future for the two of them; their lives were so different from each other. Still, it would've been nice to kiss him and quench this heightened attraction she felt for him. Her rational side was having a knockdown, drag-out with her emotional side, and she wasn't sure which one should win. One thing she did know, she needed sleep. In the morning, she'd think clearly and douse this silly, schoolgirl crush. Otherwise she was headed for trouble, because there was no way she could fall head over heels for Christian Ross. It just wasn't going to happen.

CHAPTER 8

"Well, what do you think?"

"It's incredible," Everly breathed. "More beautiful than I could have imagined."

Christian felt a burst of pride, almost as though he were somehow responsible for the view. They'd hiked to the top of Diamond Head Crater and were standing on the overlook that afforded an exquisite view of Waikiki, hugging the curvy shoreline. A line of fertile mountains embraced the city from behind. From this vantage point, the ocean was a sheet of blue glass. There were wisps of puffy clouds in the sky above.

It had been a busy morning. They'd gone to Mililani and shopped for last-minute Christmas gifts. Or rather, Everly had shopped while Christian kept the kiddos occupied. He'd promised them they would stop by Matsumotos in Haleiwa on the way back and get some shave ice. First, they needed to stop by Safeway and pick up the catered dinner he'd ordered for tomorrow. Sadie and Jordan had done surprisingly well, mostly because they were able to entertain one another. They were so excited about Santa Claus coming; it was all they could talk about. The adults milked that bargaining chip to encourage cooperation throughout the day.

Thankfully, Everly's car was untouched, luggage still in the trunk. Before Christian could take Everly to check on her car, he jogged a few miles down the road to get his SUV. He'd left it on the side of the road, the day before, when he saw Everly arguing with Briggs. And they'd walked back to the estate. In all of the commotion, he'd completely forgotten about his SUV until he went outside to get in it, and it wasn't there. A smile tugged at the corners of his lips. Everly was tangling with his mind to the point he could think of little else.

Even though it was Christmas Eve, Christian was amazed by how light-hearted he felt. He was actually looking forward to going home and spending the evening with Everly, Jordan, and Sadie. His talk with Everly in the night had done wonders, and for the first time in a long time, he felt hopeful about the future.

Admittedly, a part of him wondered how wise it was to get involved with someone who lived on the mainland, but he couldn't seem to help himself. There was something about her that had drawn him to her the first moment he saw her on the beach. The more time he spent with her, the more he liked her. She was spunky, yet refined, and he loved her adorable Southern accent.

His dad always said the first time he saw Kalena Christian's mom, he knew she was going to be his wife. Even though Christian had cared deeply for Heather, he never had a prompting that she was going to be his wife. But with Everly, he felt like it was a distinct possibility. He chuckled inwardly, grateful Everly couldn't read his thoughts. Otherwise, she'd think he was nuts. He hoped he could persuade her to stay at the estate for the duration of her vacation. She was a delicate butterfly that had graced him with her presence. If he moved too suddenly, she would lift her wings and fly away, taking her brilliant mystery with her. It was better to take things one step at a time. After all, if they were truly meant to be together, time would tell.

Christian only told a handful of people his feelings about the accident and Heather. And the few he had told looked at him with such pity he could hardly stand it. But Everly was different. Yes, she was sympathetic , but he got the impression she truly understood what he was feeling, partly because she'd also experienced a great deal of heartache.

Common sense told him it was unwise to get in the middle of Everly's dispute with her ex-husband. But he couldn't ignore the fierce need he had to protect her. Roland sounded dangerous and desperate. Otherwise, he wouldn't have sent Briggs all the way here to spy on Everly. And then there was the business about her deceased husband ... or was he still alive? It wouldn't be too difficult to ask a few questions and see what he could turn up. He couldn't imagine a guy disappearing and leaving Everly to fend for herself. She was the sort of woman that came along only once in a lifetime. The kind of woman that should be appreciated and cherished.

Everly touched his arm, amusement written on her face. "You've got some admirers."

He turned and saw a group of middle-aged women, ogling him. A constant invasion of privacy was the price he paid for fame. Still, it was hard to take sometimes. When the women realized he'd noticed them, they squealed and ran up to him. One woman was brazen enough to throw her arms around him and would've kissed him on the lips had he not averted his face.

"I just love your movies. And you're even hunkier in real life," she said, her eyes devouring him, as if he were a slab of meat. "Can I get a picture? The people back home aren't going to believe this."

Christian fixed on his movie-star smile, even though it irked him people thought they had the right to treat him like an object. "Of course."

He was pleasant as they took their pictures. Christian was about to turn away when the tall brunette leaned into his personal space, a seductive tone in her voice. "I would love to treat you to a Christmas Eve Dinner. And perhaps a little dessert after, if you know what I mean." She winked.

Christian was repulsed by the woman's forwardness and was about to politely decline her offer, when Everly stepped up and put an arm around his waist.

She flashed the women a cool smile. "Sorry girls, but it ain't gonna happen. He has other plans." She cut her eyes adoringly at Christian. "If you'll excuse us …"

The women just stood there, speechless, as Everly pulled Christian away.

Christian chuckled. "That was impressive. I should take you with me more often."

Everly scowled. "Are they always so aggressive?"

"Not all of them. But most … yes … unfortunately."

"It was disgusting how they fawned over you." She shot them a dirty look. "Vultures."

It was endearing to see Everly defending him. "People seeing me as a mere object, rather than as a person, and all wanting a piece of me has been a hard adjustment."

She shook her head. "I don't know how you put up with it."

"I'm used to it, for the most part."

Everly shuddered. "I don't think I could ever get used to that."

Christian's jaw tensed as he caught hold of Everly's arm. "Look." He pointed to a group of people hiking up the windy road to the overlook. Briggs was amongst them.

Everly's face paled. "Do you think he's been following us all day?"

"Probably." His jaw hardened. "I'm going to take care of this once and for all."

She put a hand on his chest. "Let's just go. It's Christmas Eve. I don't want to ruin it for us or the kids."

It was not in Christian's DNA to back down from anyone or anything. And he was pretty sure that Briggs had been lurking around the estate last night. One more reason to confront him.

Her eyes sought his. "Please."

"You can't let Roland keep bullying you like this. You have to face this head-on and stop it in its tracks."

Resentment flashed in her eyes. "I know what I'm doing," she snapped.

"Do you? Because it doesn't look that way from where I'm standing. The longer Roland gets away with sending his man to stalk you, the worse it's gonna get."

She tossed her head back, nostrils flaring. "You don't know what you're talking about. Don't you dare presume you know anything about the situation because you don't." She stormed away and stood with her arms tightly folded over her chest, looking out toward the ocean.

Where had that anger come from? He was perplexed by the outburst but figured there had to be more to the story than she had shared. As he stood there, watching her, he felt himself soften. Everly was such a tantalizing combination of strength and vulnerability. She intrigued him ... captivated him. He rubbed his neck and sighed, knowing he'd have to do the same thing he'd watched his dad do a thousand times with his mom—apologize in order to smooth her ruffled feathers.

He stepped up to her and cast a sidelong glance. "I wouldn't do it if I were you."

She jutted out her chin. "Do what?"

"Jump. It's not worth it."

Surprise flittered over her features, then her eyes narrowed. "I wasn't going to jump, you imbecile. But I did consider throwing your butt over."

He chuckled, loving her sharp wit. He could tell from her demeanor that her defensive shell was cracking. He nudged her. "I'm sorry."

She shook her head, her chin set defiantly.

"Really."

Her features softened. "I'm sorry too."

"Apology accepted," he said promptly. He slipped an arm around her and pulled her close. She leaned her head into the curve of his shoulder. They stayed that way for a few minutes, until Jordan climbed up on the top rung of the railing.

Everly sprang into action, getting him down. "Don't climb up there again," she cautioned.

As they made their way down the trail, they passed Briggs going the opposite direction. He was mopping his damp forehead, looking absolutely miserable. Christian straightened to his full height and kept his eyes fixed on Briggs, but the coward wouldn't even look his direction. Everly tugged on Christian's arm. "Come on. He's not worth it," she said loud enough for Briggs to hear.

Christian didn't relax until they'd gotten a good fifty yards past him. He didn't want to upset Everly, but this couldn't continue. He decided then and there that the next time Briggs or any of Roland's men set foot on his property, he was going to do a lot more than simply glare at them.

They were standing in the deli section of Safeway, and Everly couldn't believe what she was hearing. "You had your entire Christmas dinner catered ... from a grocery store?"

Christian pulled a face. "Well, it was either that or have Mele make it. I figured she would want to spend Christmas with her family, rather than cooking for mine."

"How many people are coming for dinner?"

"My mom, dad, sister, and us."

"So eight people total."

"Yes."

"And you expect to feed everyone with that?" She pointed to the small turkey and quart-sized plastic containers that had been packed up by the deli.

"Well ... yeah ... I can add some things to it, if you don't think it'll be enough."

She giggled. "I thought Hawaiians were notorious for making big meals. Where I'm from, that small amount of food would get scarfed up before you could unwrap your silverware from your napkin. Christmas dinner should be a feast."

His eyes sparked with hope. "You volunteering?"

"I suppose I could whip up a few things." The prospect caused excitement to simmer inside her. Everly's biggest reservation about spending Christmas in Hawaii was that she'd miss the traditional Christmas meal she and her mama made every year, consisting of turkey, ham, cornbread dressing, cranberry salad, mashed potatoes and gravy, country green beans, sweet potato casserole, and rolls. Everly almost had not come, but her mama assured her it worked out for the best because she wanted to spend Christmas at her sister's house in Greenville. Although, Everly suspected the only reason her mama was going to Greenville was so Everly wouldn't feel guilty and stay home. Before things unfolded with Christian, Everly had planned on finding a restaurant that served Christmas dinner. But, now, she would be able to make the food she loved ... and share a bit of her culture with Christian.

"Get whatever you need," Christian said eagerly.

"What are you planning to do for dessert?"

"Dessert?" Christian rubbed his jaw. "Ooh, I hadn't thought about that. I guess we could pick up some ice cream."

Everly wrinkled her nose. "I don't think so," she said saucily. "I'll make a pumpkin cheesecake and a crusty cherry cake."

"Wow! You're beautiful and you cook too." He pushed her arm with his finger. "Are you real?"

She laughed. "Better save your flattery until after you taste it."

CHAPTER 9

Everly breathed a sigh of relief when Jordan finally dozed off. It had been a chore to get him to sleep. She wondered if Christian was having as much trouble with Sadie. The two kids had been bouncing off the walls, so excited about Santa coming they could hardly stand it. At Jordan's insistence, they'd filled a heaping plate of chocolate chip cookies for Santa. And Sadie insisted that they needed to leave carrots for Rudolf. Christmas was magical through the eyes of children. Everly was so grateful that she had Jordan, but she often worried about him being lonely as an only child. Everly was the oldest of three girls, but she often felt like an only child because her siblings lived in other states—one in Texas and the other in Alabama. Still, she could call and talk to them when she needed a boost, whereas Jordan only had her and his momaw to keep him company. Roland would take him on the occasional outing, but since the divorce, he'd been MIA most of the time. Proof he didn't care all that much about Jordan, but was using him as a means to control Everly.

Seeing Jordan and Sadie together made Everly acutely aware of how badly Jordan needed more interaction with kids his age. And being around Christian made Everly realize how much she'd missed having someone in her life. She sighed, checking her reflection in the mirror. She fluffed up her curls and added a touch of powder to her face. She and Christian agreed to get the kids to bed and then watch a movie. The prospect of being alone with Christian sent anticipation tingling through her. Several times today, she'd felt sparks of energy when they touched, but the attraction was kept in check by the kids. She wondered if he would kiss her. Her pulse increased. It was unwise to entertain such thoughts about Christian, because the last thing she wanted was a long-distance relationship. And she didn't want to drag him into the sordid mess with Roland. Everly kept hoping and praying that Roland would find a steady girl-friend and lose interest in her. When they first got divorced, she assumed that with the passage of time, he would become less controlling and jealous. But it was turning out to be the opposite. Roland's destructive behavior was escalating. She still couldn't believe he'd sent Briggs all this way to keep tabs on her. She brushed aside the unpleasant thoughts. Regardless of what happened or didn't happen with Christian, Everly was going to enjoy tonight. She was on vacation, after all.

Everly stepped into the den, which flowed directly into the kitchen in an open-floor format. Soft music was playing in the background and Christian had dimmed the overhead lights so the lights on the Christmas tree would take center-stage. The doors and windows were open, allowing a pleasant breeze to flow through. There were a few presents under the tree, but they'd agreed to wait until later to put out the Santa gifts. Christian was in the kitchen. He turned when he saw Everly.

"I'm heating up a pot of water for hot chocolate. Do you want anything to munch on?"

"Popcorn would be good. Do you need any help?"

"I think I can handle it." He flashed a lopsided smile, which exposed his dimple. "You've been cooking all afternoon. The least I can do is make you some hot chocolate and popcorn."

"I would like that," Everly replied as butterflies fluttered through her stomach. He really was gorgeous.

After returning from the grocery store, Everly had set to work making the desserts for tomorrow. She'd also baked cornbread for the dressing and assembled the sweet potato casserole. She wanted to get most of the prep over with, so she wouldn't be rushed tomorrow. Everything was ready to go into the oven at this point. Thankfully, Christian had ordered a pizza for dinner, and they set out store-bought cookies for Santa. Christian had thanked her a dozen times for cooking; but the truth was, she enjoyed it. Cooking was relaxing and helped bring a sense of normalcy to the situation, especially when she made items so integral a part of her heritage.

She sat down on the plush leather sofa. A couple of minutes later, Christian came in carrying a large bowl of popcorn. He placed it on the coffee table and sat beside her. "So, what movie do you want to watch?"

A smile played on her lips. "How about an action movie?"

He made a face. "Really? I figured you'd want to watch a Christmas movie. I have *It's a Wonderful Life*."

"Nah, I prefer to watch something a little more exciting."

"Okay, exciting's good." He reached for a handful of popcorn and shoved it in his mouth. "Let's see what I've got in the queue."

"How about *Freefall*?"

He jerked around. "What?"

"*Freefall*. You know, the action movie starring ..." she put a finger to her forehead, feigning thinking ... "Sorry, I can't remember the guy who starred in it."

His face fell. "You're not really gonna make me watch that with you, are you?"

"Why not?" The prospect of watching his own movie made him squirm, which made it all the more fun to tease him. A curl had slipped into the middle of his forehead, giving him a boyish look that was so intensely attractive she could hardly think straight. Her fingers itched to thread through the thick tangle of curls. "You don't like the movie?"

"Yeah ... it's okay. I don't like watching myself. It's weird."

She gave him her best puppy-dog look, batting her eyelashes. "Please?"

He sighed. "Okay ... for you."

The water kettle whistled. Christian hopped up. He returned carrying two mugs of steaming hot chocolate.

Everly took a sip. It was every bit as good as it had been the night before.

Christian started the movie. When he appeared on screen, Everly whistled and cheered, loving how color seeped into his face. Somehow, despite the stardom, Christian retained a healthy level of humility. And Everly found that very attractive. With Christian sitting right next to her, it was hard to focus on the movie. Her pulse bumped up a notch when he slipped his arm around her. She leaned into him, liking how nicely her head fit into the curve of his shoulder.

About a fourth of the way into the movie, Everly turned to him. "You really are a great actor. I know you said you were semi-retired, but are you planning on doing more movies in the Jase Scott series?"

"I'm not sure," he said evasively, his eyes going a shade darker.

Instantly, she picked up on his hesitancy. "Why wouldn't you? You're a natural-born actor."

He removed his arm, a guarded expression coming over his face.

Everly knew she was prying. And if her mama were here, she'd remind Everly it wasn't ladylike to press Christian into talking, but she couldn't help herself. It seemed like such a waste of God-given talent for Christian to give up acting. She placed a hand on his arm. "I'm sorry, I didn't mean to intrude in your personal affairs."

He let out a long breath. "No, it's a fair question. And the answer is ... I'm not sure if I'll ever go back to that life again." His eyes deepened, fathomless in their intensity. "Too many memories."

Even though she was just getting to know Christian, she couldn't help thinking he was hiding out here on this estate, letting life pass him by. It was sad. Then again, who was she to judge? She'd spent the last 2 ½ years dodging Roland.

His lips pressed into a tight line. "Don't look at me like that."

"Like what?"

"Like you're disappointed."

She was surprised he'd read her so accurately. "I'm not disappointed ... exactly. It's just hard to see someone casting aside a gift. She pointed at the TV. You're good. And, please forgive me for saying this, but you're not doing yourself or anyone else any favors by running away."

He bristled. "You don't know what you're talking about."

She arched an eyebrow. "Then maybe you should explain it to me."

His eyes went hard. "It's awfully easy for you to sit there and cast judgment on me, when you're cowing to Roland."

The words were a slap in the face. She took in a ragged breath. "You know what? This is a mistake. I shouldn't be here." She stood.

He jumped up. "Now who's the one running away?" He caught her arm. "Tell me why you let Roland run all over you."

She glared at him. There was something cathartic about the intensity building between her and Christian. Most of the time, she plastered on a friendly smile to the world, while bottling up her feelings. But she truly wanted Christian to know where she was coming from, and she wanted to understand him. "Okay, but only if you'll tell me why you stopped acting."

They stood there, staring at each other, until Christian relaxed his shoulders. "All right." A ghost of a smile stole over his lips as he touched her hair. "At least you didn't tell me to 'stick it where the sun don't shine' this time."

Her hands went to her hips. "Well, I would, if I thought it would help," she retorted, but all she could think about was his nearness. She wanted to throw her arms around him and kiss him until her need subsided.

He chuckled. "I don't doubt it. Shall we sit back down?"

She sat down and crossed her arms tightly over her chest. She cut her eyes at him. "You first."

"Okay, here goes. I miss acting ... more than you can imagine." His eyes took on a faraway look. "Being on the set is invigorating. When

I'm playing a part, it's like I'm becoming that person. And Jase Scott is larger than life. There's nothing he can't do. Anyway, you get the point." He paused. "When I got my first big break, I thought I had it made. I was walking on air and nothing bad could touch me. But then the accident happened. And when Heather died ..." The words caught in his throat, and he coughed. He sighed heavily and began again, clasping his hands together. "When Heather died, everything changed. Life turned dark, and I felt like I was caught up in a never-ending wave, rolling so fast it would consume me. One night, in particular, I felt like I couldn't go on." His voice broke, and Everly placed her hand over his. He swallowed. "I found myself on my knees, praying for help ... begging for a sliver of light to direct my path. It was at that moment that I had the distinct impression I needed to go home." He offered a grim smile. "And I've been here ever since."

She let that sink in. "Have you been off the island since you came back?"

"No."

Her brow creased. "You know, just because you received the impression to come home doesn't mean that you have to give up what you love."

He nodded, but she could tell from the pain in his eyes that he didn't believe that. "Here on the estate, I have my privacy. You saw how those women acted at Diamond Head and how people stared at us at the grocery store. Everywhere I go, I'm in a fishbowl." He rubbed his eyes. "It's hard enough to deal with a tragedy, but try dealing with it while the whole world is watching. I just don't think I can go back to that again."

"I understand."

He cocked his head. "Really?"

"Really. I'm sorry you had to go through that. I suppose that's why they say life is a four-letter-word."

He frowned. "What do you mean?"

"You've never heard that before?"

"No."

"In the South, we call curse words four-letter-words."

Realization dawned as he laughed. "Ah, makes sense. Yes, I suppose life is a four-letter-word sometimes."

"Yep. But we have to keep living it anyway."

"Indeed."

"It's like the poem *Anyway* by Mother Teresa." She could tell from his blank look that he'd never heard it before. From the time she was a little girl, Everly's mama had quoted the poem. "It's kind of long, but the gist of it is this:

> *What you spend years building, someone could destroy*
> *overnight;*
>
> *Build anyway.*
>
> *If you find serenity and happiness, they may be jealous;*
>
> *Be happy anyway.*
>
> *The good you do today, people will often forget tomorrow;*
>
> *Do good anyway.*
>
> *Give the world the best you have, and it may never be*
> *enough;*
>
> *Give the world the best you've got anyway.*
>
> *You see, in the final analysis, it is between you and*
> *your God;*
>
> *It was never between you and them anyway.*

He grew thoughtful. "I like that. Good words to live by."

"Yep. As a kid I always added my own lines.

"You may be the shyest kid in the room, but you need to act confident anyway."

Christian chuckled. "You? Shy? I don't believe it."

"You know the saying—fake it till you make it. That's my mantra."

"Well, it obviously works."

"Of course, my mama was the queen of adding in her two-cents to the poem. Her favorite when I was a teenager was. 'You may not like cleaning your room, but you need to do it anyway.'"

"Smart mom."

Everly felt a rush of tenderness for her resilient mama who'd survived her husband walking out on her when Everly was a baby and cancer too. "Yeah, she's pretty great."

"I'd like to meet her sometime."

Time seemed to slow as their eyes locked. This relationship was progressing at warp speed. In many ways, it felt like she'd known Christian forever. A part of her wished she and Jordan could stay here in his world. "I would like that very much," she uttered.

Tenderness filled his eyes, and she saw the longing he felt for her. He probably would've kissed her, had she not scooted backwards.

He looked surprised and a little hurt, but she needed to know something before this went any further. "You must've loved Heather very much." The words spilled out between them like lava burning a chasm between adjoining mountains.

His jaw started working. "I cared a great deal. Heather was a free spirit, only living for the moment. Everything with her felt fleeting and temporary. I suppose, in time, I would've come to love her ... if the situation had been different."

Silence overtook them, each of them lost in thought, until Christian spoke. "Seeing Heather in a wheelchair ... knowing she would never be able to walk again or have a normal life ..." His voice caught. "Every time I looked at her, I kept thinking—why her? Why was I okay when she wasn't?"

The anguish in Christian's voice was heartbreaking, and Everly wished she had the words to ease his pain. All she could do was nod and let him know she understood.

"I-I should've been there for her." He balled a fist and brought it to his mouth.

"I don't understand. It sounds like you were there for her. It's not your fault. It was an accident, and you weren't even the one driving."

"I went to visit Heather often, but it was painful and awkward. Heather resented the fact that I was virtually unscathed, while she was paralyzed."

"She said that to you?" she said, feeling a sting of anger at this woman she'd never met.

"No, she never voiced it out loud, but I could see it in her eyes. She forced an argument about something silly." Regret clouded his eyes. "I knew what she was doing, and honestly, I was relieved because it gave me an excuse not to see her as often." His voice grew hoarse. "The last time I visited her she was frustrated and bitter." His eyes grew moist. "I knew she was hurting, but I didn't know how to help. She told me she couldn't live that way, but I didn't catch the meaning of what she was saying. I was too caught up in my own turmoil to see things clearly. And it cost Heather her life."

Everly cupped Christian's jaw. "Look at me." When he turned to face her, the tortured look in his eyes nearly carved out her heart.

She dropped her hand, letting it fall back into her lap. "No one gets a free pass from adversity." She jutted out her chin. "No one. You didn't know that Heather was going to commit suicide. Yeah, maybe you should've visited her more often, but it sounds to me like you did all you were capable of doing at the time. You don't know what was going through Heather's mind or the depth of her pain. But I would venture to say if Heather were here today, she'd tell you to stop living a life of regret. You've mourned enough. It's time to put aside the past and move on. Heather would want that."

He blew out a breath. "I'm trying. I try every day."

A tight smiled formed over her lips. "Okay, then that's that."

He shook his head. "What?"

"If you're doing your best, then so be it."

He cocked an eyebrow. "Are you using reverse psychology on me?"

"Nope. I'm simply stating that if you're truly doing your best, then you shouldn't have any regrets."

"Easier said than done," he grumbled.

She looked him in the eye, not backing down an inch. "Even though you feel like giving up, you have to keep moving forward anyway."

He chuckled softly. "A new line to your poem?"

"Yep."

She cut her eyes toward the Christmas tree. "Here's another line —even though Everly and Christian have their own set of issues they're dealing with, they're gonna put them aside tonight and enjoy Christmas Eve anyway."

"Good idea." He leaned forward, his voice husky. "And how do you suggest we do that?"

"I think you know," she said softly.

Her breath caught when he trailed a finger along the curve of her cheek, sending delicious tingles spiraling down her spine. His lips were soft and welcoming as they moved with hers in a perfect dance that encapsulated her in a sense of belonging, And she had the crazy impression she was coming home to a place where she belonged. Then he deepened the kiss, sending a rush of energy through Everly that turned her bones to liquid. She let out a tiny moan as she threaded her fingers through Christian's hair. Christian slipped his arms around her waist, pulling her closer as she melted into him. They kissed until she was sated with passion, to the point where she could hardly think straight. When he pulled back, they were both breathing hard.

He rested his forehead against hers. "That was amazing," he murmured, a smile playing on his lips. "See, even IZ agrees."

"IZ?"

"The song ... *What a Wonderful World*."

"Oh, the song." She'd been so caught up in Christian that she'd forgotten there was music playing in the background." She laughed. "What song?"

His eyes danced. "Exactly. This is turning out to be a great Christmas Eve, if I do say so myself."

"No, you're wrong," she said with a deadpan expression.

Uncertainty crept into his eyes. "What?"

"It's not Christmas Eve anymore." She couldn't stop the smile from spreading over her lips. "Merry Christmas."

His eyes lit up. "And so it is. Merry Christmas," he uttered, before his lips took hers.

Briggs pressed his face to the window, grateful that Christian didn't have any security cameras or guards. Otherwise, he never would've been able to get this close to them. As it was, he'd followed them all over this stinking island. The hike up Diamond Head had about done him in, but Roland had ordered him to keep a close eye on them. And he'd been able to snap a couple of pictures with them standing close together. But this. This took the cake. He leaned closer, watching the two of them kiss. He'd never pegged Everly as being overly smart, but the woman was stupider than he thought. This was not going to end well. Once Roland got wind of it, there would be no end to his wrath. Everly's little fling with the movie star would most likely cost the poor sap his life. And it would be Everly's fault. She knew better than to anger Roland this way. When it came to Everly, he wasn't rational. In Roland's mind, once Everly accepted his hand in marriage she'd become his property. Nobody messed with Roland's property and lived to tell about it.

On a personal note, Briggs wasn't too happy with Everly, because he'd been forced to follow her here. Thanks to Everly, Briggs was spending Christmas alone ... on this remote island where it was hot and muggy, the opposite of a traditional Christmas with snow and a cheerful fire that warmed the bones. He hated the ocean almost as much as he the hated sand. About the only thing Briggs had to look forward to this holiday season was the six-pack of beer he had stowed away in the tiny refrigerator in his hotel room. The sooner he got this over with, the sooner he could get back there and relax. He lifted his iPhone and began snapping pictures.

CHAPTER 10

"Mommy!" Sadie bounded into Kat's arms as the two embraced.

"I missed you," Kat said. "This trip was too long."

Christian was surprised by the momentary pang of sadness he felt. Witnessing the exchange between mother and daughter, he was reminded that even though he and Sadie were super close, she wasn't his child. Being a devoted uncle wasn't the same as having his own children. Furthermore, spending time with Everly made him keenly aware of how boring his life had become. Now that she'd come into his life, he didn't want things to go back to the way they were before.

Sadie took Kat's hand and led her over to the presents, which took up the bulk of the den floor. "Look what Santa brought," she exclaimed, her eyes shining with excitement.

"Wow, Santa brought you lots of presents. You must've been a good girl."

Sadie nodded. "Uh, huh."

"Thank you," Kat mouthed to Christian. Because Kat had been out of town for most of the month, Christian had done all of the Christmas shopping.

He winked. "No problem."

Kat sat down in a chair and crossed her legs. "You put up a tree this year."

"Yeah, I couldn't let Sadie spend Christmas without a tree."

"I'm glad."

Jordan came running into the room. He was holding a toy car in his hand and making a zooming sound. Sadie giggled and began running behind him. Kat's eyes grew round. "Who is that?"

"Jordan."

"Where did he come from?"

"It's kind of a long story."

"Spill it," Kat ordered, finger-combing her short hair. But before Christian could speak a word, Everly stepped into the room, looking gorgeous in a red V-necked shirt and jeans that hugged her slim figure. Kat's jaw dropped as Everly smiled and extended her hand.

"You must be Kat. I'm Everly. It's nice to meet you," she said in a smooth, polished tone.

"Nice to meet you too," Kat said. She turned to Christian for an explanation.

"Everly's my ..." he hesitated, suddenly realizing he didn't know what to say. She wasn't his girlfriend, but she felt like she was so much more. Color seeped into his face as he looked to Everly for help.

"My son Jordan and I are on vacation here," Everly explained, "and your brother was kind enough to invite us to Christmas."

Kat's eyes danced as she shot Christian an appraising look. "I see. Well, it's very nice to meet you, Everly."

The doorbell rang, and Christian went to answer it.

Minutes later, Christian's parents entered the room in a flurry, their arms loaded with presents. They placed them under the tree and hugged Sadie and Kat. Then they spotted Everly and everything stilled.

A similar scene was repeated as Everly introduced herself. Then Christian's parents looked to him for further details.

"Everly's here on vacation from South Carolina. I invited her to have Christmas with us." He gave Everly a look of encouragement and went to her side to prevent her from feeling uncomfortable. A few minutes later, he realized his worry was in vain, for Everly was perfectly capable of holding her own. She and Kat struck up a conversation and began chatting like they were old friends. Everly seemed to know all the right things to say, and before long, his entire family was enthralled with her.

Christian's mom Kalena inhaled appreciatively. "Something smells good."

"Everly's cooking us some Southern food," Christian said, feeling a touch of pride.

"Southern food, huh? By a Southern Belle. I'm looking forward to that," his dad said. "I was worried we'd be forced to eat that bland food from the grocery store we had last year."

Christian's face fell as Everly laughed. She wagged a finger. "See, I told you that you couldn't serve that slop for Christmas dinner."

"Hey, it's not my fault Mele insists on taking off Christmas."

"Everly, we're certainly glad you're here," Kat piped in. "And our stomachs are especially grateful." Everyone laughed as she continued, "Stay as long as you like."

"Thank you," Everly said. "The food's in the oven and should be ready in about twenty or so minutes. As a matter of fact, I'd better check on it."

Christian's response was immediate. "Do you need any help?"

"That's okay, I've got it," Everly said, casually touching his arm. "I know you want to catch up with your family." She rewarded him with a brilliant smile that melted his insides. Being with Everly made him feel like he was ten years old again and seeing his first Ferrari. Now that he'd met her, he couldn't imagine going back to his ho-hum life.

Kat waited until Everly was in the kitchen before whispering to Christian. "I like her."

"So do I," his mom said decisively.

Always the practical one, his dad chuckled. "Take it easy, girls. Their relationship's only getting started, and you're already marrying them off."

"Oh, shush," Kalena said, patting his leg. "You know I have a sense about these things. She's very beautiful, with those bright eyes and long curls." She winked at Christian. "Promise me, you won't let her get away."

He laughed, feeling a burst of happiness that filled his entire chest. "I'll see what I can do."

———

Everly thoroughly enjoyed spending Christmas with Christian and his family. They'd devoured nearly every bite of her food and from the way they kept going on about it, Everly would've thought she was a five-star chef. It was very kind and flattering. After dinner, they piled into a couple cars and drove to the beach where they walked along the shore and let the kids play in the sand. Jordan was sad that Sadie went to her own home with her mom. But Kat promised to bring Sadie back the following day, so that helped take the sting out of the situation. Later that night, after everyone left, Everly put Jordan to bed and assumed she and Christian would hang out in the den and watch a movie like they'd done the night before, but Christian had other plans. He insisted they put on their suits and go for a late-night swim. At first, Everly balked at the idea because she didn't want to leave Jordan in the house alone. But Christian assured her he would be perfectly safe. He even pulled out an old baby monitor that he'd used with Sadie and brought it to the pool, so they could hear if Jordan woke up.

Everly had to admit, the evening swim with Christian was one of the most thrilling things she'd ever done. Her fascination with Christian seemed to be growing the more time she spent with him. She loved his gentle manner and how he was genuinely interested in what she had to say. They had in-depth conversations, ranging from politics to spiritual topics. And the physical aspect of their relationship was like experiencing constant fireworks. Her skin tingled at his very touch, and when they kissed, her black-and-white world turned to glorious color. They rounded out the evening by getting in the hot-tub and enjoying long kisses that left her breathless. And then he did something that completely took the wind out of her sails.

Christian cupped her cheek, looking so deeply into her eyes that she swore he could see into her very soul. "Stay with me," he implored.

"What?"

"Don't go back to Charleston. Stay here with me. We can build a wonderful life together."

The promise in his eyes was so enthralling that for a moment, she believed she could stay here. But then she thought about her mama ... her job ... Roland. "I wish I could stay," she said wistfully.

"You can."

"I could never leave my mama. She depends on me."

"She could come here."

"You've never even met my mama. For all you know, she could be nuts."

He chuckled. "Is she like you?"

"A little."

"Then I'll love her."

The implication of his words hit Everly with enough force to nearly take her breath away. Was he suggesting that he loved her? No, that was impossible. They'd not known each other long enough to fall in love. And yet ... he was asking her to come here and live. And she desperately wanted to. "My job."

"What about your job?"

He lightly traced the outline of her collarbone, driving her to distraction.

"I've worked so hard to get where I am. In a few years, I'll be able to buy into the club and be a part owner."

He looked thoughtful. "Okay, I'll buy you a workout center ... if that's what you want."

She laughed. "Sure, if only it were that easy." Then she saw his face. "You're serious." It boggled her mind that he was wealthy enough to purchase a fitness center on a whim.

"Absolutely." His expression grew earnest. "Look, I know this is all sudden, but I can't deny how I feel about you." He pulled her close and gave her a long, tender kiss. He pulled back, searching her face. "I know you feel the same way."

"Yes," she admitted. "I wouldn't be here with you if I didn't."

He smiled. "Good. It's settled."

Her head started spinning and she felt like she'd been dropped in the middle of the ocean without a life preserver. "What? No, it's not settled. I can't just drop everything and move here." A mere week ago, she'd been living a normal life, never dreaming in a million years that she'd be here ... with Christian Ross. Maybe this was all a dream, and she would wake up to find she was back in Charleston ... all alone and living in Roland's shadow. She backed away from him. "It's all happening too fast. We're just now getting to know each other."

"I'm not asking you to marry me ..." a lopsided smile curved his lips "...yet."

The promise of what he was saying sent a thrill rushing through her. "But you're asking me to move here and run a fitness club for you."

"I'll get you and Jordan a place nearby, and we'll get to know each other."

She rubbed a hand across her forehead. Suddenly, the hot tub felt scorching hot, and she could feel sweat popping across her forehead. The hope in his eyes was so tempting that she almost threw caution to the wind and told him yes that very instant. But this situation was too reminiscent of Roland. He'd swept in on a white horse and rescued her from all of the problems that resulted when Mitchell died ... err disappeared. And that was another thing, she'd come here to find out about Mitchell, and Christian was distracting her from that. "I'm sorry. I can't commit to that right now." She looked at him, her eyes pleading.

He nodded, his lips forming a tight line. "Is it because of Roland?"

"Yes, partly."

His jaw hardened. "What hold does he have over you?"

"Jordan," she said simply.

"I don't understand. Jordan's not even his flesh and blood."

She collected her thoughts, trying to find the best way to describe the situation. "Roland' s a high-power attorney. Not only does he know the ins and outs of the law, but he has a great deal of influence over the lawmakers in Charleston." Her eyes clouded as she voiced her greatest fear. "I don't want him to take Jordan away from me."

Christian shot her an incredulous look. "I would imagine that it would be almost impossible to separate a mother from her child."

She let out a harsh chuckle. "Yeah, one would think, but you don't know Roland. He's wicked-smart and manipulative. And he'll stop at nothing to get what he wants." Even as she spoke the words, a sense of foreboding crept over her. She dreaded the repercussions that were sure to follow when she returned from this trip. Heaven forbid if Roland realized how she felt about Christian.

"You can't spend the rest of your life walking on eggshells around the guy. Has he threatened to take Jordan away from you?"

"Not in so many words, but the implication's always there."

"If he tries anything, then we'll get an attorney and fight him."

Christian's argument sounded so logical, but there was no way to explain Roland's ruthless nature.

"If you're worried about the money ... don't."

Gratitude welled in her breast, and she could hardly believe this wonderful man was real. Her eyes misted as she touched his face. "I appreciate the gesture ... more than you could ever imagine, but I can't drag you into my crazy life." She swallowed the emotion, fighting to keep her tears at bay.

He put a hand over hers. "Let me love you, Everly. Give me a chance. I promise I won't let you down. Will you at least consider it?"

The hope simmering in his eyes cut her to the quick. "Okay, I'll give it some thought" she said, guilt pelting over her. There was no way she could come here and be with Christian. Roland would never allow it. He would destroy them both and take Jordan from her. And no matter how captivated she was with Christian, she was not willing to put Jordan at risk. What Christian didn't understand was that things didn't work out as nicely in the real world as they did in the movies.

Relief settled into Christian's eyes. "I can live with that ... for now."

CHAPTER 11

"Man, it's great to hear from you. How long has it been? Four years? I suppose it's hard to find time for your old friends now that you're a big-time actor."

"Yeah," Christian said, "things have been sort of crazy the last few years."

There was an awkward pause and then Luke swore under his breath. "Aw, man, I'm sorry. I shouldn't be bagging on you. You've had it pretty rough. Do you ever see Vic or any of the other guys?"

"No, I haven't." Luke was referring to the group of guys that Christian and Luke used to hang out with in high school when they played football at Kahuku. For Christian, those days seemed like another lifetime.

"We had some good times, didn't we?" Luke said.

"Yeah, it was great." He launched into his topic before Luke could venture too far down memory lane. "Hey, listen, the reason I'm calling is because I have a friend who's needing information on her former husband. And I know you have the inside scoop at the police department."

He chuckled. "I don't know about that, but I'll certainly help you anyway I can."

"I really appreciate that." Christian told him everything he knew about Mitchell Grant. "Does that name ring a bell?"

"No ... sorry, dude. I can ask around though. See what I can find out."

"According to a private investigator named Benny Kai, the guy was using an assumed name."

Luke let out a low whistle. "Are you talking about the Benny Kai that was killed?"

Christian sat up straighter. "Could be. How did he die?"

"He got mixed up in a case involving an art dealer that was crooked. Some guys came looking for the dude, and Benny got caught in the crossfire." Luke paused. "This guy, Mitchell Grant ... he wasn't an art dealer, was he?"

"I'm not sure. Why?"

"Because Cooper Stein was an alias the art dealer was using."

Christian's pulse bumped up a notch. "Is Cooper Stein still on the island?"

"No, he was killed by the same guys that killed the P.I. My partner Kalia worked the case. Supposedly, this guy, Cooper Stein, hid a truckload of art and antiquities somewhere on the island. The dude even had a Rembrandt that he stole from a museum. The Rembrandt was returned to the museum, but no one has found the stolen art."

Christian had not thought to ask Everly what Mitchell did for a living. At present, she was in the pool with Jordan. "Hang on a sec. Let me ask my friend what her former husband did for a living."

He found Everly lounging in a chair while Jordan swam. "Hey, I'm on the phone with my detective friend from the police department, asking about Mitchell. What did he do for a living?"

"He owned an art gallery."

Christian's stomach tightened as he nodded.

Everly sat up, concern etching her features. "Is everything okay?"

"I'll explain in a minute."

"Luke? You still there?"

"Yep."

"My friend's former husband owned an art gallery."

"Oh, boy. Do you think it's the same person?"

"I'm not sure." Christian tried to keep his expression passive, so he wouldn't alarm Everly. "Can you text me a picture of him?"

"Yeah, give me few minutes."

"Thanks, man. I owe you big time."

Luke laughed. "Nah, small kine. That's what friends are for." He paused. "Hey, can you let me know for sure if this is your guy? I know Kalia would be interested to know. Her best friend almost married Cooper Stein."

"Sure will. Thanks." Christian ended the call.

Everly's face had gone pale. "Does he know anything about Mitchell?"

"I'm not sure. He's sending me a picture of a guy named Cooper Stein. It may be Mitchell." He didn't dare mention that Cooper Stein was dead.

Everly nodded, her features tight.

Five minutes later, Christian's phone buzzed. Even as he pulled up the photo, his heart dropped. The picture was a spitting image of Jordan. He handed Everly his phone. "Is this him?"

Tears pooled in her eyes. "Yes." Her hands started to shake. "Mitchell's not dead. All this time, he's been living here." Anger flashed in her eyes as tears rolled down her cheeks. "How could he do that to me? To Jordan?"

He hated to tell her the rest. "I'm afraid there's more."

"What?" she barked.

"Mitchell's dead. He was killed a few months ago."

Her face crumbled as she let out a cry. Christian gathered her in his arms and held her close as she wept.

———————

As luck would have it, the guy from *Introspective Magazine* showed up half an hour later to do the interview. In all of the commotion, Christian had completely forgotten he was coming. Christian, Everly, and

Jordan were still out by the pool. Everly's tears had dried, but she was stoic and withdrawn.

Christian was surprised to see a man striding across the yard towards them. He tensed. "Do you recognize that man?"

Everly looked. "No."

"Do you think it's one of Roland's men?"

"I'm not sure ... I've never seen him before."

Christian stood as the man approached and extended his hand. "Hello, I'm Bart Smith from *Introspective Magazine*."

The reporter's keen eyes moved over Everly and Jordan. Christian cringed inwardly. The last thing he wanted was to put Everly and Jordan in the spotlight, but their association with him would do just that. Unfortunately, there was nothing he could do at this point but move forward with the interview and hope for the best. He pasted on the friendly smile he wore when dealing with the press.

"Come on inside." He looked at Everly's pinched expression, wishing he could comfort her. *Of all the lousy times for a reporter to show up.* "This interview won't take more than thirty minutes, tops, and then I'll be back out."

Everly hugged her knees to her chest and nodded.

The reporter's face fell. "Thirty minutes? I'm supposed to do a full interview about your home and lifestyle. It's not possible to limit it to thirty minutes."

Christian eyed the man. "Unfortunately, due to circumstances beyond my control, thirty minutes is all we've got. I suggest we make the most of it," he snapped.

Bart sighed heavily and pushed his glasses up higher on his nose. "So be it."

Christian gripped the steering wheel and cast a sidelong glance at Everly. "Are you sure you're up for this?"

Everly nodded, her lips forming a tight line. Ever since she'd found out about Mitchell, a curious numbness had settled over her.

She was still trying to come to terms with the fact that he'd deserted her and Jordan. He'd never even once come back to see his own son. What kind of man did that? She was starting to wonder if she'd really known Mitchell at all. And on top of that, he was murdered ... only a few months ago. She wasn't sure what she was feeling, because she thought she'd closed that chapter of her life many years ago. And here she was again ... back at square one. She could tell Christian was worried about her. He'd been a great help with Jordan, entertaining him so she could have some time alone to sort things out.

Once Christian's friend at the police department realized Mitchell and Cooper were indeed the same person, he connected them with the woman Mitchell had almost married. And she agreed to meet with Everly at her home at Turtle Bay Resort. She, Christian, and Jordan were headed there now.

Christian grabbed her hand and squeezed it. She was so grateful for him and his kindness. He was fast becoming a large part of her life, and she didn't want to think about leaving him. But what other choice did she have? She'd not gotten a single call or text from Roland since the day before Christmas Eve, when she'd hung up on him. Instinct told her that was a bad thing. She kept bracing herself for the firestorm that was sure to come. Was Briggs still lurking about the island, keeping tabs on her? A shiver ran down her spine as she looked at the blue expanse of ocean and the foamy white waves. Oahu was breathtakingly beautiful, but she'd barely had a moment to enjoy her surroundings. Soon she would be back home, and this place ... and Christian ... would be a memory. Without warning, tears emerged.

As they turned into Turtle Bay, Christian noticed she was wiping her eyes. "Are you okay?"

She nodded. He assumed she was upset about Mitchell ... and she was, but the tears were for him. Her feelings for Christian were running deeper than she could've imagined.

"This is it," Christian said when they pulled in front of a particular condo.

Everly turned to Jordan in the backseat. "I need you to be a big boy for Mommy, okay? Can you do that for me?"

"Okey dokey," he chimed.

Everly held her breath as Christian punched the doorbell. He gave her a nod of encouragement and slid an arm around her.

The door opened to reveal a pretty redhead with hair as curly as Everly's. A warm smile on her face. "Hi, I'm Maurie."

"I'm Everly." Jordan was standing directly in front of her. She squeezed his shoulders. "This is my son, Jordan."

"Hi, Jordan."

Maurie's smile faltered a notch when she saw Jordan. It was to be expected, considering Jordan was the spitting image of Mitchell.

"Hello," Jordan said in a grownup voice.

"Hello. Please come in." Maurie stepped back and let them enter. She motioned to the sofa and chairs. "Have a seat."

Everly and Christian sat on the sofa. Jordan was just climbing into Everly's lap when a small dog trotted in. Jordan jumped up and down, his eyes lighting up. The dog made a bee-line for him, and he dropped to his knees and began petting it.

Maurie laughed. "It looks like Rebel's made a new friend." She looked at Jordan. "She really likes you."

"I like her too," Jordan said.

It wasn't until Christian placed a hand over hers that Everly realized she'd been wringing her hands. He gave her a nod of encouragement, causing emotion to well in her breast. She swallowed it back down, trying to gain a measure of control. Coming here was harder than she imagined. She took a deep breath. "Thanks for letting me come and—"

A guy came in from the back. He smiled as he stepped up to them. "Hi, I'm Liam, Maurie's husband," he said, extending a hand to Everly first.

"It's nice to meet you," Everly said mechanically.

When Liam went to shake hands with Christian, his jaw dropped. "You're Christian Ross."

Christian chuckled. "Guilty as charged."

Liam pumped Christian's hand up and down. "Well, isn't this just the bee's knees! I love your movies."

Maurie laughed. "I can attest to that. I can't count the number of times Liam has made me sit through *Freefall*." She held up a hand to Christian. "No offense, but after the hundredth time, it starts to lose its luster."

Christian shook his head. "None taken."

Liam swiped his hair from his eyes and perched on the arm of the chair in which Maurie was sitting. He draped an arm around her. "Now, that's hitting a little below the belt, love. We don't just watch *Freefall*. We also watch *Lethal Target* and *Crossfire*."

"Uh, huh. See what I mean," Maurie chirped.

"Ask her how many times she's made me watch *The Tourist*," Liam said.

Maurie rolled her eyes. "Not nearly as many times as we've watched the Jase Scott movies. I can promise you that."

Liam's eyes twinkled as he grinned. "Women. Can't live with them. Can't live without them."

Maurie lightly elbowed him, but judging by her grin, it was obvious that she was more amused by Liam's antics than annoyed. Everly decided then and there that she liked the two of them ... a lot. Despite their teasing, she got the feeling they were super close. She was a little envious that Maurie had been able to put her life together so quickly after Mitchell or Cooper's betrayal and then death. *If only she were as resilient.*

Liam looked at Jordan. "And who might this young chap be?"

"I'm Jordan," he said matter-of-factly.

Liam chuckled. "Indeed you are."

"Hello," Jordan said, his eyes going back to Rebel.

Maurie nudged Liam. "Maybe you should take Jordan and Rebel outside to throw the ball. That way, Everly and I can have our little chat."

He sprang into action. "Good idea."

Jordan stood, his eyes dancing with excitement. He clapped his hands. "Come on, Rebel."

Christian squeezed Everly's knee. "I think I'll join them." He gave her a tentative look. "If you're okay with that."

"Of course. Thank you."

After the men left, Maurie scooted in her seat, getting comfortable. "I thought it would be better for us to discuss this privately, without little listening ears."

Everly was grateful Maurie was so intuitive. She didn't know how much of the conversation Jordan would comprehend at his age, but it was better to be safe than sorry. "Thank you." Everly scooted to the edge of her seat. "And I really do appreciate your willingness to talk to me."

"You're very welcome. Let me begin by saying I'm sorry for your heartache."

The compassion in Maurie's eyes evoked tears. Everly blinked them away as she nodded. "Thanks," she gulped. "How much of my story did you hear?"

"Not much, I'm afraid. Just the highlights. I know you were married to Cooper and that he faked his death."

"Yes, that's the gist of it. He was going by the name Mitchell Grant at that time. We'd only been married a few years, but things were rocky. You see, I'd accidentally gotten pregnant with Jordan, and Mitchell resented it."

Maurie's lips puckered in disapproval. "That's too bad."

"He went on a diving trip to Lake Tahoe and never came home. I, like everyone else, assumed he was dead. We even had a funeral for him." Anger surged through Everly as she clenched her fist, digging her fingernails into the palm of her hand. "And then a few months ago, a friend of mine saw Mitchell at a restaurant when she was here on vacation."

"Yes, I remember. We were eating lunch at Bubba Gump Shrimp when she approached our table. Cooper pretended not to know her, of course. Claimed she'd mistaken him for someone else."

"A short while later, I received a call from a private investigator named Benny Kai. He told me that he suspected Mitchell was alive and using an assumed name. He asked me to send a photo, which I did. But I never heard from him again. I've since learned that he was killed."

Maurie shifted in her seat. "Yeah, I'm afraid that came about because Liam suspected that Cooper wasn't what he was claiming to be. He hired Benny." She paused, regret tingeing her features. "But he never imagined it would lead to Benny's death."

"So the men that killed Benny were looking for Mitchell ... um ... Cooper?"

"Yes, the men were art thieves. Cooper hired them to steal paintings from a museum in Boston. The deal went wrong, and Cooper shot the ringleader's brother. So he came looking for Cooper." Maurie hesitated, and there was a slight tremor in her voice when she continued. "The men who killed Cooper would've killed me and Liam ... had Liam not saved me. He took a bullet for me and was shot in the shoulder."

"Wow! I didn't know. I'm sorry. I'm glad you're both okay."

"Thank you."

So, you and Liam knew each other while you were engaged to Mitchell?"

"Liam and I have been best friends and business partners for years, but only just got married four months ago." She placed her hands reverently over her belly, her face glowing. "And I just found out a few days ago that we're going to have a baby."

"Congratulations. It's obvious from the way Liam looks at you that he adores you. You're very lucky."

Maurie nodded. "Yes, I am. Very blessed." Her eyes met Everly's. "And from what I saw earlier, I'd say that you and Christian are also very blessed."

Everly began blinking rapidly. "We only just met a few days ago. We barely even know each other."

"That doesn't matter. When you find the right one, you know."

"Well, that's just it, I thought I knew that Mitchell was the right one." Her eyes flashed with resentment. "And we see how that turned out. At this point, I don't trust my own judgment when it comes to men." Tears pooled in her eyes.

Maurie grunted. "You don't need to doubt yourself because you were bamboozled by Cooper ... or Mitchell ... whatever the heck his name was. I think I'm as level-headed as the next person, and he fooled me. He was a con artist. He fooled everyone."

Everly wiped away the tears rolling down her cheeks. If only it were that simple. First Mitchell and then Roland. And she was still dealing with the fallout from the latter.

"Look, I can't even begin to imagine what you must be going through. You loved Cooper. He was the father of your child."

"It's just hard to wrap my mind around the fact that Mitchell was alive all those years."

"I understand. But the sting will ease with time ... it always does. And in the meantime, you have your whole life ahead of you and—" Maurie stopped midsentence and pointed. "Look."

Everly turned. She didn't see what Maurie was referring to at first, but when she craned her neck and looked at an angle, she could see past the kitchen to the double sliding-glass doors that opened to the backyard. Liam was pitching a ball to Jordan. Christian was standing directly behind Jordan, his hand resting on Jordan's shoulder as he instructed him on how to catch it.

Maurie continued. "Someone very wise once said, 'Don't let the past hold the future hostage.' Every once in a while, amidst the doubt and pain, life gives us those little nuggets of gold. But we have to have enough sense to reach out and grab them."

This time, Everly allowed the tears to flow freely down her cheeks as she turned back around.

Maurie smiled. "I believe you've found your happy ending. Don't let it get away this time."

CHAPTER 12

Everly slipped the straps of the sundress over her shoulders. It was cherry red with large, white, hibiscus flowers. She liked how the vibrant color set off her tan. She wondered if Christian would like it. Next, she applied her eye makeup and blush. A shimmery lip-gloss added the final touch. She fluffed her curls and allowed them to fall loose on her shoulders. Most of the time, she lived in yoga or spandex pants due to her profession. Since she'd been on Oahu, she'd been wearing shorts and t-shirts, except for the one day when she wore jeans to Diamond Head. It felt good to get dressed up.

After the initial visit with Maurie and Liam, Everly and Christian went to dinner with them the following evening, while Mele babysat Jordan. Liam kept them laughing with his witty jokes, and Everly found his British accent charming. Maurie, on the other hand, was full of practical advice and wisdom. Spending time with them, seeing the life they'd built together, gave Everly a glimpse of hope for her and Christian. She was tired of living her life in the shadows, fearing Roland's every move. A new year was upon her and it was time to make a change.

Her phone buzzed. She reached to answer it. "Mama, how are you?"

"Great, darling. Charlotte and I spent the day shopping and then we stopped by the grocery store to pick up a few things. We're making our traditional New Year's Day meal tomorrow."

Everly made a face. "I'm sorry I'll miss that."

"I know you're on vacation, honey. But it might be wise to try and find some collard greens and eat at least one bite tomorrow."

Her mama was a stickler for tradition and felt like it wasn't possible to ring in the New Year without having a ham hock, black-eyed peas, collard greens and cornbread. Legend had it that if you ate these items you would be blessed with good fortune during the upcoming year. Peas symbolized coins and the greens folding money.

Everly laughed. She could only imagine the look on Christian's face if she told him she had to hunt down a can of collard greens to make sure she had good fortune the upcoming year. "Yeah, I'll see what I can do."

"Well, it certainly can't hurt. You don't want to jinx yourself," her mama countered, a hint of reproof in her voice, suggesting she didn't appreciate Everly laughing about it. "So, how are you and Jordan doing? Are you enjoying the beach?"

"Yes, we are." She'd not told her mama about Christian initially, because she didn't think the relationship was going anywhere. But, the past couple of days with him had been glorious. They'd not talked about the future or what would happen when she went home. Rather, they had gone to the beach—played in the waves, taken long walks, and built sandcastles with Jordan and Sadie. Everly couldn't remember ever being this happy. It was time to come to terms with what was happening here. She had strong feelings for Christian and couldn't imagine him not being part of her life. There. She admitted it. Now it was time to break the news to her mama. She drew in a deep breath, trying to bolster the courage to say the words aloud. Her mama hadn't cared much for Mitchell, and she detested Roland. She would understandably be leery about Christian, especially since he was a superstar. "Mama, I met someone."

Silence.

"He's really great." The words spilled out as she blabbed on about how he helped her and Jordan during the tsunami. "Actually—" she forced a light laugh "—we've been staying with him at his estate."

"What? You're staying with a man you hardly know?"

She cringed at the shocked tone in her mama's voice. "I know, it sounds crazy. And it caught me off guard too. But when you meet him, you'll understand."

Her mama began firing questions at her. "But what will you do when the vacation's over? Will he move to South Carolina? Will you move there? What about Jordan? Is he good with him?"

Everly pulled her fingers through her hair. "He's great with Jordan. And I don't know the rest." She didn't dare bring up the fact that Christian had offered to buy her a fitness center to run ... here on Oahu. She didn't want her mama to blow a gasket. She'd take things one step at a time. Maybe she could go back to South Carolina for a few weeks and then bring her mama here to meet Christian. Ease her into the idea.

"Does Roland know?"

The question caused a knot to form in Everly's stomach. "Um ... I —I'm not really sure how much he knows at this point."

"What do you mean?"

"He sent a guy here to follow me."

The only sound over the phone was the sudden intake of Florence's breath. Finally, she spoke. "This is getting scary, Everly. It's time to go to the police."

If only that were an option. "Roland has the Charleston police in his pocket. Going to them will only incite him, making things worse than they already are."

"You don't know that for sure."

"Yes, I'm afraid I do."

"What's Roland going to do when he finds out about this new guy?"

The trepidation in her mama's voice caused goose bumps to rise over her flesh. "I don't know. But Christian's different."

"Different ... how so?"

She thought about how easily Christian had put Briggs in his place. And how he had the means to combat Roland legally. Although, she didn't want to put Christian in the middle of a battle between Roland and her. *Not the smartest way to start a new relationship.* Still, it might come to that. Everly's instinct told her she would be safe with Christian. But she didn't want to voice that out loud to her mama, for fear of sounding hokey.

"Promise me you'll take things slow with this new guy ... Christian. You're just now coming to terms with Mitchell's betrayal. You need to be smart. For Jordan's sake."

"I am being careful." Irritation prickled over Everly, even though she understood where her mama was coming from. She'd told her about Mitchell the day she found out. The interesting thing was her mama wasn't the slightest bit surprised. If anything, she felt vindicated because she'd never really liked Mitchell, but couldn't put her finger on why.

"So, is Christian from Hawaii?"

"Yes, he's half Tongan and half white."

"What's a Tongan?"

Everly laughed. Her mama had only stepped foot out of South Carolina twice in her entire life, and her world view was the size of a pea. Not that Everly faulted her for that. She was salt-of-the-earth and had been Everly's saving grace for the past few years. "Tonga is a country in the South Pacific."

"Oh."

"What does he look like?"

This is where it got tricky, but there was no way around it. She had to tell her mama who he really was. "He's Christian Ross." She braced herself for the backlash that was sure to follow.

"Okay. But that doesn't tell me anything about him or what he looks like."

"Mama, he's the Christian Ross." She could tell her mama was clueless. "The actor? That plays the action hero Jase Scott."

"Never heard of him," her mama said tartly.

Everly couldn't believe what she was hearing. She assumed everyone had heard of Christian Ross. Then again, if it wasn't *Bill*

O'Reilly, Fox News, or *The Price is Right*, her mama didn't watch it. "He's a famous actor."

"So, you're telling me you're staying at the home of a famous actor?"

"Yep."

"And you really like him?"

"Yes," she said softly. "I like him a lot."

"Oh, boy. This is not going to end well with Roland. I have a bad feeling about this."

Her eyes narrowed as she gripped the phone tighter. "I can't keep letting Roland control my life, Mama. It's time I stood up to him. Once and for all."

"Yes, you're right. I just worry about Jordan."

"The best thing I can do for Jordan is to give him a stable environment, with a man who truly cares about him." Even as she spoke the words, an image of Christian and Jordan flashed through her mind. She saw them in Maurie's backyard, playing catch.

"Don't you think things are moving too fast? You've only just met Christian."

Everly's neck and shoulders suddenly felt tight. "I'm not going to rush off and marry him. We're only dating."

"Have you thought about the repercussions of dating someone famous?"

She sighed. "Not really."

"Well, you should think about it. I've seen the way reporters hound actors. You'll never have a minute's peace."

Sometimes her mama reminded her of Chicken Little, always waiting for the sky to fall. "I guess I'll just have to take it one step at a time."

"But—"

Now, Everly was tired of discussing it. Her mama's doubts were raising too many doubts of her own. "I've gotta go. I'll call you tomorrow. Love you."

"Okay. But I'm concerned."

"I know. But it'll be okay. I promise. Gotta go," she said hurriedly. "Love you. Bye."

"Bye," her mom said as Everly ended the call with a heavy sigh. The last thing she wanted to do was worry her mama, but she was glad her relationship with Christian was out in the open. And once her mama met him, she would love him just as much as Everly did. She stopped. Had she really just thought the word *love*? It was way too soon for that. But her feelings for Christian ran much stronger than mere *like*. She was crazy about him. Okay, that was better. She would go with *crazy about him* ... for now.

CHAPTER 13

Originally, Christian had planned on taking Everly and Jordan to the Polynesian Cultural Center to see the night show *Ha: Breath of Life* so they could see the fire-knife dancers. But, as luck would have it, Jordan began complaining of a tummy ache around 4:00 in the afternoon. At first, Everly thought he might've eaten too much candy. But when he vomited, she realized it was an illness—most likely a virus. Mele went to the store to get chicken noodle soup, crackers, Gatorade, and popsicles. Jordan was starting to feel better, but not well enough to go out in public. Mele had offered to stay with Jordan, so Christian could take Everly to the night show. But Christian could tell she wanted to be with her family on New Year's Eve. Christian didn't blame her. Mele was so good to him that he didn't want to abuse her kindness. Besides, Jordan was looking forward to seeing the fire-knife dancers, and Christian didn't want him to miss out. So, he decided to do the next best thing—bring the party to them. Thankfully, Mele helped him pull everything together, before she left for the evening.

Christian hoped Everly would like it. In a way, it was better the way it turned out because Christian would now be able to share a bit of his growing up years with Everly. He'd made a point of not pressing her about the future, but as her departure date from the island drew closer, he was getting concerned. Life was rich and full with Everly, and he didn't want to go back to the way things were before. He could only hope and pray that she cared as much about him as he did her.

That day on the beach, when he first met Everly, he was having a particularly hard time dealing with Heather's death. So, he decided to take Sadie to the beach in order to clear his head. And then he saw Everly. From the first moment he laid eyes on her, he was so acutely aware of her presence that she was all he could think about. And then when he ran out of sun block, he felt like it was a sign he should talk to her. When she gave him a good tongue-lashing in that cute Southern accent, he was smitten. She'd pulled him into a pool of intoxication, and he'd not come up for air since. Maybe he was more like his dad than he realized. He was beginning to think love at first sight was very real.

It didn't bother him that Everly had a few personal things to work out in her life. He, of all people, knew the harsh blows that life dealt. It was hard to see Everly hurting over Mitchell's betrayal, but that was easier to come to terms with than Roland because it was now behind them. Roland was another story. Everly was scared of the man. Christian could hear it in her voice ... see it in her eyes. And it infuriated him so much he hired a private detective to check into Roland. It certainly couldn't hurt to know what he was up against. Of course, he hadn't mentioned that to Everly. There was no use upsetting her. She had enough to deal with as it was.

Christian did a double-take when Everly emerged from the house and glided across the patio to the thatched-roof pool house where he was standing. Her hair bounced softly on her shoulders, and she was the picture of grace. She caught his eye and smiled, sending his heart into a tailspin. When she stepped up to him, he encircled her waist and leaned in, kissing the delicate part of her neck. Her clean hair smelled of fruity shampoo. His gaze flickered over her, lingering on her bright eyes, which seemed to hold the mysteries of the universe within their golden rims. It was crazy how a delicate little thing like her had the power to consume him.

She motioned at the table, which was laden with kalua pig, salmon, rice, baked sweet potatoes, mango slices, and pineapple. A glass vase of red ginger flowers in water adorned the center. "Wow! This looks amazing."

The soft glow from the tiki torches flickered against her face, adding a touch of mystery to her features, and he had the feeling his entire life was culminating into this moment.

A smile tugged at his lips. "Since we couldn't go to the PCC tonight, I thought I'd bring the party to us anyway."

She gave him an appraising look. "Now that's putting Mother Teresa's poem to good use." When she went to sit down, he moved into action, pulling back a chair. "Allow me."

"Thanks," she said, her eyes caressing his.

He swallowed, feeling a bit like a sixteen-year-old on his first date. Christian sat across from Everly. "Where's Jordan?"

"I told him he could watch TV. He's feeling much better." She laughed. "At this point, he's milking the sickness for all it's worth, eating as many popsicles as he possibly can."

Christian grinned. "You can't blame a guy for that." Even though he was super fond of Jordan, he was immensely pleased that they would be able to share a meal together, just the two of them. He reached for her hand and looked into her eyes. "Thank you."

She cocked her head. "For what?"

"For being a part of my life."

Her eyes misted as she smiled. "It goes both ways."

After they'd eaten, Christian scooted back his chair. "Okay, it's time to go and get Jordan." When Everly gave him a questioning look, he flashed a mysterious smile. "The night's just beginning. There's something I want to show you."

She stood. "Okay, I'll be right back."

By the time she returned with Jordan, Christian had lit the ends of the wooden baton and was twirling it around in a circle at a rapid-fire pace.

Jordan's eyes lit up as he jumped into the air and squealed. "Mommy! Look! Christian's twirling fire."

Even though it had been years, the baton flowed through Christian's hands effortlessly, finding its place as the light from the fire blazed around him. Finally, when he was finished, he tucked it under one knee and raised both hands in the air.

Everly and Jordan sprang to their feet, furiously clapping.

Christian removed the baton and bowed.

"That was awesome," Everly beamed. "I didn't realize you could do that."

"I paid my way through college, working at the Polynesian Cultural Center, before I went to L.A. I was one of the fire-knife dancers."

Everly pointed. "I don't see any knives," she teased.

He winced. "Yeah, it's been a few years since I've twirled, so I thought I'd better not tempt fate."

She stepped up to him and held out her hand. "Do you mind if I give it a whirl?"

He quirked a grin. "I dunno. That might not be such a good idea. You don't want to light your hair on fire."

She placed a hand on her hip, arching an eyebrow. "Give me the dang baton."

Reluctantly, he handed it over and was shocked when she started twirling it. Even though the baton was too long for her, she maintained good control. He held his breath when she tossed it in the air. And then, when she actually caught it, he knew he'd met his match.

She winked and handed it back to him, a pleased expression on her beautiful face. "Back in South Carolina, where I come from, the women twirl fire."

––––––––––––––

Long after the New Year's Eve countdown was over, Everly and Christian sat out by the pool, letting the coolness of the evening envelope them. Everly scooted closer to Christian, her head resting in the curve of his shoulder. She looked up at him. "This was the best New Year's Eve I've ever had."

"Me too," he murmured into her hair.

She linked her fingers through his, liking how nicely they fit together. "I don't want this to end."

He shifted so that he was looking into her eyes, hope coloring his features. "Are you saying what I think you're saying?"

A smile broke over her lips as happiness bubbled over her. "Yes."

His eyes lit up as he let out a *whoop*. He pulled her to her feet and gathered her close. "You have no idea how happy that makes me. Listen, they're playing our song."

"Our song?"

"*What a Wonderful World* by IZ." He grinned. "It's appropriate, yeah?"

A smile curved her lips. "Totally," she said softly. "It is a wonderful world when we're together."

He leaned close, nuzzling her ear with his lips. "I'm crazy about you, Everly."

Tingles danced down her spine. "I'm crazy about you too."

As they started swaying along to the music, Everly's mind started clicking through the details. She would have to go back to Charleston and wrap up her business affairs. Maybe rent out her house. Put in her notice at work. Deal with Roland. She stopped. "Are you sure you're ready for all that this will entail? I have to have a way to make a living for Jordan and me."

"Of course," he said smoothly. "Whatever you need." He twirled her in a circle and began humming along to the music.

She planted her feet on the ground. "I'm serious. I have to work. If I can run a fitness center for you, that would be ideal. Are you still okay with that? I have some money saved up that I can invest in it."

There was the faintest hint of amusement in his eyes. "That's not necessary. I have plenty."

"I know, but I need to be able to stand on my own," she countered firmly. "Contribute my fair share." She'd made the mistake of letting Roland handle everything for her after Mitchell's disappearance, but she wouldn't make that same mistake again. She was going to come into this relationship on equal footing or not at all.

He chuckled. "We can arrange it however you want."

"I just want to make sure we have everything ironed out before I go home and put in my notice."

His eyes caught hers, and she had the impression she was seeing into her future—a wonderful future that she could grow accustomed to. "I gave you my word, and that's not something I take lightly."

Gratitude welled in her breast, and she had to fight to stay the tears. "That means the world to me," she said quietly.

He searched her face. "Are you okay?"

"Yeah, this is all just so sudden. I'll have to break the news to my mama. She won't be happy about me taking Jordan five thousand miles away from her."

He thought for a minute. "She can come here too."

"Really?" Was this all just a wonderful dream? It felt that way, especially since she was standing in such a beautiful spot and breathing in perfumed air from the nearby flowers. A salty breeze floated gently in the night air.

"Of course. Everly, I want you to be happy. We can do this. We'll take it slowly and work our way through it ... one day at a time. If need be, I can even go and spend some time with you in South Carolina."

She was surprised. "But that would mean leaving the island."

"Really? South Carolina's not on the other side of the island? I didn't realize," he teased.

She stuck out her tongue. "Smarty pants."

A mischievous glint flashed in his eyes. "Let's see ... I think this calls for adding a new line to poem ... Christian's scared stiff to step foot off the island, but for Everly, he'll do it anyway."

"You'll do just fine," she assured him. Her mind jumped ahead to the next problem as she chewed on her inner jaw. "What about Roland?"

He stiffened. "What do you mean?"

"He's not gonna take it lightly when he realizes I'm leaving

Charleston and taking Jordan with me." A sense of foreboding trickled through her as she shivered.

His eyes hardened. "Like I said, we'll take it one step at a time and work through the kinks. You can't keep letting him rule your life."

She straightened her shoulders, remembering the advice Maurie had given her. Life was giving her a nugget of happiness, and she was grabbing hold and never letting go. "You're right." She just hoped Christian realized what he was in for, because even though she wasn't sure what Roland would do when he found out she was moving to Hawaii to be with Christian, she knew things were going to get a whole lot worse before they got better.

CHAPTER 14

The last few days of Everly's vacation were spent planning. She decided to wait until she returned to the fitness center to deliver her notice in person. Matt, the owner, had been so kind and generous to her—offering her every opportunity for advancement—she felt she owed it to him to tell him in person. She and Christian went house hunting. Everly wanted to rent a home, but Christian insisted they would be smarter to buy something. Everly contacted Maurie and told her the plans. Maurie was elated that Everly and Jordan would be returning to the island. A day later, she called and offered to let Everly rent her and Liam's condo.

"We've been planning on buying a home before the baby comes," Maurie explained. "We just found the perfect house and were planning on renting out our condo. If you want it, it's yours."

Everly couldn't believe how smoothly things were working out.

"It's because it's meant to be," Christian told her.

They were in Christian's SUV, headed to the airport, but first they were stopping to eat lunch. The only thing that took the sting out of leaving Christian was the knowledge that she and Jordan would be back in less than a month. Christian wanted to go with her to South Carolina, but Everly insisted it would be better for her to go home alone and sort things out. It would be hard enough for her mama to come to terms with all of the changes. Having Christian present would add extra stress. And aside from that, there was the obvious part about him being a movie star. Everywhere they went, people clamored for his attention. Everly wasn't sure how she felt about that, but was willing to take things one step at a time.

They decided to stop at a McDonalds, so they could get to the airport in time. Everly had just lifted Jordan out of the car seat when they were attacked by a pack of reporters. Microphones were thrust in her face as people closed in around them.

"Everly, tell us how it feels to be the newest woman in Christian Ross's life."

"Mommy," Jordan cried, burying his head in Everly's shoulder.

Everly saw Christian's furious expression as he rushed around the car and began pushing his way through the reporters to get to her side.

"How did you feel when you realized your ex-husband, Mitchell Grant, didn't actually die in a diving accident?"

Everly felt like she'd been punched in the face.

"How does your son feel about having his father desert him?" This came from a pretty blonde in her early twenties.

Anger seared through Everly, and she was about to tell the reporter just what she thought of her nasty comment, but a magazine was thrust in her face. "What do you have to say about this, Ms. Watson?"

It took a second for Everly to process what she was seeing— pictures of her and Christian, kissing in the hot tub, their bodies intertwined. Horror rushed over her as she read the caption: Christian Ross gets in on the action.

"Where was your son when you and Christian were in the hot tub? Was someone watching him, or was he in the house alone?"

A swift panic raced over Everly, and she had the feeling the ground was falling out from beneath her.

"Sources tell us that you and your son have been staying at Christian Ross's estate. Is this true?"

Jordan started crying. Christian made it to her side. "Leave her alone," he ordered. "You're scaring her son."

They turned on Christian.

"Does your developing relationship with Everly mean that you've finally gotten over Heather's suicide?"

"Do you still feel responsible for Heather's state of mind?"

"Will you be doing another movie in the Jase Scott series?"

Christian's jaw went rock hard. "I have no comment. You're upsetting my friend and her son. I would ask that, in the name of decency, you leave us be."

This provoked more questions. It all became a blur to Everly as Christian took Jordan from her arms. He opened the car door, placed him back into the car seat, and helped Everly get in.

The reporters hovered over the SUV, beating on the windows and firing more questions at them. Everly had the impression they were hungry wolves, fighting for a piece of fresh meat. Christian got into the car and started the engine. It was only when he slammed the SUV in reverse and backed up that the reporters were forced to move away.

When they got onto the highway, Christian shook his head. "I'm so sorry. I don't know what that was all about."

Everly spun around. "How dare you!"

Christian rocked back, gripping the steering wheel. "What?"

"*Introspective Magazine*. That's the one you did the interview for, right?"

"Yeah. So?"

Tears sprang to her eyes. "They have pictures of us ... kissing in your hot tub."

"What?"

"And they know about Mitchell." This was a nightmare.

He swore under his breath, gripping the steering wheel. "Calm down. I'll call my agent and find out what happened. It was only supposed to be a lifestyle segment."

She belted out a hysterical laugh. "It was a heck of a lot more than that. And no, I won't calm down. I've never been so humiliated in my life."

"Welcome to my world," Christian muttered darkly.

The tawdry image of Christian and her in the hot tub was seared into her mind. The reporter had asked her where Jordan was when she and Christian were kissing ... and if she'd left him alone. She could only imagine the repercussions that would follow when Roland caught wind of this. Her hands started to tremble as she clasped them tightly in her lap.

Christian blew out a breath. "Hey, I'm sorry." He reached for her hand, but she pulled it away, then turned and stared unseeingly out the window. "Everly," he continued, "we need to talk about this."

She merely shook her head.

"Unfortunately, what you experienced today goes with the territory. I don't like it any more than you do."

Fury boiled inside her. "Did you tell that reporter about Mitchell?"

"Of course not. How can you think I would do that?"

"And yet they knew," she spat back.

"You're overreacting, Everly."

Tears spilled over her cheeks. Maybe she was overreacting, but she couldn't live like this.

"We need to discuss this," Christian said.

"I'm sorry." She bit her lower lip. "But I can't do this."

His face fell. "This will blow over."

"They took pictures of us ... together ... insinuated I'm a neglectful mother. What part of that do you not get? Do you know what Roland will do when he hears about this?"

"Will you stop it, already? This isn't about Roland! It's about us."

"Don't you see? There can't be an *us*. Not now." She folded her arms over her chest. "I was foolish to think there could ever be."

Shock rendered him speechless for a second. "Everly ... don't do this! That incident with the reporters was nothing ... small kine."

She shot him a look that could kill. "Well, it was a big deal to me."

"So, that's it? You're throwing away what we have—what we can build together—over something stupid?"

Tears blurred her vision. "I don't want to talk about this right now."

"Fine." Christian's mouth formed a hard line. "You accused me of running away from my problems, but from where I'm sitting, it looks like you're the one who's running away."

Her lower lip quivered. "Just take us to the airport ... please."

"I trusted you, and you hung me out to dry." Fury brought bitter bile into Christian's throat, making it difficult to swallow. If Boston were standing in front of him, he would've knocked his lights out.

"Whoa, man. Take it easy," Boston said.

"The interview was supposed to be a simple lifestyle segment," Christian shouted, pacing back and forth in front of the pool.

"Yes, that's what we agreed on. I've already called *Introspective Magazine*. The editor apologized profusely and promised to fire the reporter."

"That's not good enough!" Christian wanted to wrap his hands around the reporter's skinny neck and squeeze until his glasses popped off his face. "I never should've trusted you, Boston," he said hoarsely. "How did the reporter find out about Mitchell Grant? The only people who even knew about him were the detectives. I called Luke, my contact on the police force, he swears they didn't breathe a word."

"I don't know, man. Looking at all of the pictures of you and Everly, I can tell you that something's fishy. Some of them were taken inside your home."

Christian's blood ran cold. "What? He'd stopped looking at the magazines and Internet days ago, because it was too painful. The media had taken something beautiful and was turning it into sleaze.

"You and Everly are in the living room on the couch. Someone was spying on you, watching your every move. And this media frenzy

... I've been at this game a long time, and I'm telling you, man, this is not normal. Someone has to be fueling this. Think. Who has an axe to grind ... against you or her?"

Christian drew in a ragged breath. It had been right in front of him the whole time, but he'd been too caught up in the turmoil to see it.

"Talk to me, dude. Do you know who could be doing this?"

"I'm going to have to let you go."

"Wait!"

Christian ended the call, and then kicked a lounge chair, sending it flying across the concrete.

Kat, who was sitting in a nearby chair, jumped back, her hands in the air. "Whoa. Easy! Does Boston know who's doing this?"

Rage stormed over him. "No, but I have a pretty good idea who it is."

Kat stood. "Okay, but you need to calm down. Take a deep breath. Let's talk this thing through. Figure out what to do." She cocked her head. "Who's doing this?"

"Roland," he seethed.

"Who?"

"Everly's ex-husband. She tried to warn me about him, but I downplayed it." A tortured look came into his eyes. "I assumed I could handle anything he could dish out."

"Are you positive it's Roland?"

"About ninety percent."

"Okay." She put her hands on her hips. "You need to find out for sure. Is there a way to do that?"

He rubbed a hand across his neck. "Yeah, I hired a P.I. to find out about Roland, but I haven't followed up with him yet. I've been too preoccupied with all this other stuff to even think about it."

"All right. Call and find out." Christian moved to make the call, but she caught his arm. "Hey, I want you to do something for me." She paused, eyeing him.

What?"

"You love Everly, and she loves you. The two of you are good together."

He grunted. "Try telling Everly that. I can't get her to answer my calls or texts. At this rate, I'll probably never see her again."

She lifted an eyebrow. "Oh, just stop it, already!"

He rocked back. "Stop what?"

"Feeling sorry for yourself. You've been moping around here since she left."

His eyes narrowed. "What else am I supposed to do?"

She flung her hands in the air. "More than this! You're Christian Ross, for heaven's sake." She tapped her temple. "Think. There's got to be something you can do. Use your connections to benefit you for once, instead of hiding out and waiting for the reporters to take advantage of you."

Christian's first inclination was to lash out at Kat, tell her she didn't have a clue what she was talking about. But deep down, he knew she was right. Kat had a knack for making the best out of any situation. She'd pulled herself up by the bootstraps after a painful divorce, which in and of itself was impressive. Then, she went on to build a hotel empire.

"Go and get your woman," Kat said, a fierce look in her eyes. "And if this guy, Roland, is the one behind this you need to expose him."

Kat made it sound so simple, but it was just the pep-talk he needed to jumpstart him into action. He tried to think—connections? What connections could he use? Then it came to him like a bolt of lightning breaking through leaden clouds. And he knew exactly what he needed to do.

CHAPTER 15

Everly walked stiffly past the group of women, keeping her head held high, even though she wanted to wither up and die. They were gossiping about her and Christian. In fact, it had gotten so bad at the fitness center that Matt called her into his office the previous day, expressing concern that it was hurting the image of the center.

"If you weren't such a good manager, I would consider letting you go over this scandal," he said. "We can't have all these reporters lurking around here, snapping pictures of you. It's not good for business."

Her first impulse was shame. But thankfully, the anger took hold as she told him in no uncertain terms that her only faults were trusting a con artist and falling for a movie star. "I've been loyal to you, Matt. And patient. You've been promising for years to bring me in as a partner. In fact, most of your clientele was built by me. I work harder than anyone else here, and I ask for very little." She looked him in the eye. "The least you can do is to stand by me now."

He squirmed in his seat. "Well ... um ... yes ... you have worked hard. And I appreciate everything you've done to build this business. I will support you, but we've got to make sure these reporters don't scare away our customers."

"I'm sure it'll blow over soon," she assured him, even though there didn't seem to be a snowball's chance in Hades of that happening. Reporters thronged her wherever she went, even stooping so low as to set up camp outside her mama's house the night before last. The whole thing was absurd. All of this because she'd been stupid enough to fall for a movie star. Geez!

Every aspect of her life with Mitchell was being unearthed by reporters. And that bled into her relationship with Christian. She'd even gotten a visit from a representative of the life insurance company that had paid the policy on Mitchell's death. That's the part that unnerved her the most. Were they going to demand that she pay back the money? There was no way she could do that. She'd be sunk for life! The long arm of Mitchell's treachery was with her still.

Christian kept calling and texting, but she'd not responded. She missed him like crazy and regretted that things between them had ended the way they had. Several times, the urge to respond to him was so strong she could almost taste it. But giving him hope that they could build a relationship would be cruel, because there was no way she could live the rest of her life under a microscope. Hopefully, all of this would blow over the moment the reporter sharks caught wind of fresh blood in another direction.

Jordan kept asking to play with Sadie. And several times, he asked when Christian was coming to visit. "He's teaching me to play catch, Mommy," he said proudly. Hearing the adoration in Jordan's voice as he spoke of Christian was salt in the wound. She was grateful Jordan was young. Hopefully, he wouldn't be tarnished by the ugliness of all that was happening.

As Everly pulled into the carline of the preschool, she surveyed the area hoping there weren't any reporters present. Otherwise, the school might tell her that Jordan could no longer attend here. The last thing she needed was to have to find him another school right now. As far as she could tell, the coast was clear. Her shoulders relaxed as she moved along the line, waiting her turn. Fifteen minutes later, when she pulled up to the school, Jordan's preschool teacher approached the car. Everly looked past her to the line of children, waiting for their parents. Where was Jordan? Her heart started to pound as she rolled down the window.

"Hello, Miss Watson." She smiled politely. "Was there something that you needed?"

"My son," Everly said, wondering why the woman was asking the obvious.

The young teacher's smile fell a notch. "He's not here."

Alarm splattered over Everly, rendering her weak. "Well, where is he?"

"Mr. Watson picked him up during lunch."

Everly's face drained. "What?"

The teacher looked concerned. "I'm sorry, I assumed you knew."

The words bulldozed over Everly as she shook her head. "Thank you," she mumbled as she rolled up her window and sped away. Her mind was on fire as she fumbled in her purse for the phone.

Roland answered on the third ring.

"Where's Jordan," she demanded, fear rising thick in her throat.

He laughed. "What? No *hello*? Or how are you? I mean, it's been what? A week since you got home from your trip?"

"Stop it, Roland. You had no right to take Jordan without my knowledge. Where is he?"

"Take it easy," he said in a friendly tone, but she caught the blade in his voice. "Jordan's fine. He's right here with me. Say hello to your mom."

"Hi, Mommy," Jordan chimed.

Tears splashed over Everly's cheeks. "Hi, honey," she said, trying to keep the panic out of her voice. "Where are you?"

"Daddy took me to get ice cream! I got strawberry, and it was so, so good."

Roland came back on the line. "We're at my place now. Why don't you join us for dinner? We have much to discuss."

It was a summons, rather than a request. "I'll head there now," she said, determined to get to Jordan as quickly as possible.

"No need to rush, darling," he said breezily. "Take your time. We'll be here."

Her skin crawled. Roland hadn't called her *darling* since their divorce. What game was he playing?

"See you soon," she barked and had almost hung up when she realized Roland was speaking.

"Oh, and by the way, from the looks of the pictures I saw in the rag columns, it looks like you worked up a nice tan in Hawaii. I'm looking forward to seeing it in person."

The innuendo in his voice turned her stomach sour as she ended the call and threw it back in her purse. She cursed under her breath. The anxiety came a minute later, tightening her throat. She could tell from the smug tone in Roland's voice that he knew he had the upper hand and was going to use it to his full advantage. How could she have been so stupid? She'd let her guard down with Christian, allowed her heart to overrule her good sense. And now she was going to pay dearly for it. Heaven help her!

Roland was all smiles when he answered the door. Everly pushed past him and rushed into the living room to get to Jordan. He was lying on the sofa with his legs crossed, watching TV. She sat down beside him, relief spilling over her. "Hey, bud." She ruffled his hair. "How was school today?"

"Okay," he shrugged, turning his attention back to the TV.

"Let's get your shoes on. Momaw's at our house. She's expecting us to have dinner with her."

Roland leaned against the door frame, his arms folded, eyes veiled. "You can't leave."

The deadly calm tone of his voice left no room for argument, chilling her to the bone. Her instinct was to grab Jordan and get as far away from Roland as she could, but she knew it was crucial to keep her cool. She met his gaze. "I'm sorry. I've already made plans with Mama."

He ignored the comment. "That was an interesting development about Mitchell." When she didn't answer, he continued. "I realize now that you went there searching for him. I'm not sure how that makes me feel, actually."

She couldn't give a flying flip how it made him feel, but she didn't say as much. It was hard enough dealing with Roland as it was. No sense adding fuel to the fire. The whole blasted world knew the intimate details of her life, because it was being broadcast on every available media channel. She'd felt so sorry for Christian because his personal life was put under a microscope, and here she was, facing the same thing ... because of her association with him. Very ironic. At this rate, she wouldn't be the least bit surprised if the media started broadcasting the status of her bowel movements.

"You should've come to me for help. I would've helped you search for Mitchell."

She glanced at Jordan. "I'd rather not talk about this right now."

"I can only imagine the turmoil it must've caused you to know that Mitchell faked his death and was living another life. You finally found him, only to learn that he really was dead." He shook his head. "Tough luck."

It was just like Roland to kick her when she was down. "It's been a long day. And we need to be getting home. My mama's waiting for us."

He waved a hand in dismissal. "She'll be okay. This is important, and we're going to have our talk. Let's go in the kitchen." He looked at Jordan. "Unless you'd rather have the conversation right here."

She felt like she was being led to the firing squad as she stood. Roland walked beside her. "You look beautiful," he said, his dark eyes trailing over her. He touched her arm. "You always did look spectacular with a tan." She sat down and folded her arms tightly over her chest, glaring at him. This was Roland's little charade. It was up to him to speak first. She assumed Roland would sit across from her and about freaked out when he sat so close their legs were touching. He took her hands in his.

"I've missed you," he said softly.

She had to fight the urge to laugh in his face. Admittedly, he was a handsome man with his dark eyes and chiseled features, which is what initially drew her to him. But he did nothing for her now. If anything, she was repulsed by him. On the surface, he oozed charisma and charm, but inside he was cold and selfish. She removed her hands from his. "Don't."

He scowled. "Don't what? Talk to my wife?"

"Ex-wife." Every conversation with Roland was doomed to take a nosedive, so she might as well get all the ugliness out in the open, here and now, and save herself the trouble of tiptoeing around it. "You had no right to go to the school and get Jordan without my knowledge."

"If I want to pick up my son and take him out for ice cream, then that's my privilege. We have joint custody, remember?"

Technically Roland was right. But he played that card only when it suited his purpose. There had to be some way she could get through to him—make him understand where she was coming from. Surely he had a shred of decency somewhere in his wretched body. "Roland," she began, trying hard to keep the anger out of her voice, "I need to know where Jordan is at all times. Please don't ever do that again."

His eyes turned to flint. "Yeah, I see how concerned you were about our son when you were in the hot tub with Christian Ross."

She had the urge to rush at him, claw the smug expression off his face. "That's none of your business."

His cold eyes cut into her. "On the contrary, you and Jordan are my primary business."

"You had no right to send that thug to Hawaii to follow me."

"And you had no right to take my son to Hawaii without my knowledge."

"He's not your son," she fired back and then regretted it instantly when she saw the fury on his face.

He grabbed her arm. "Let's get one thing straight. You and Jordan belong to me."

The ruthless look in his eyes sent a shiver of fear running down her spine. "Roland, you're hurting me."

He let go and drew in a labored breath, like he was trying to gain control of his emotions. A second later, he was all charm and smiles again. "I get it. You were upset about my relationship with the other woman. So you went to Hawaii to blow off a little steam and hooked up with Christian Ross. You paid me back. Hit me where it hurts. It's time to move on and put the past behind us."

Her jaw dropped. Was he really narcissistic enough to think her relationship with Christian had anything to do with him? Furthermore, his reference to the "other woman" was absurd. There'd been so many women she couldn't possibly count them all. Even though she knew it was smarter to just keep her mouth shut, the words issued forth nonetheless. "Do you really think you can compare your numerous affairs with my relationship with Christian?" A hysterical laugh bubbled in her throat. To be such a smart attorney, Roland certainly wasn't the sharpest tool in the shed when it came to relationships. Then again, he was most likely just toying with her.

He looked puzzled. "Of course. I stepped out on you, so you stepped out on me."

"You and I aren't married anymore." Indignation buzzed through her as she stood. "I don't owe you a blasted thing."

Roland's voice grew silky smooth. "Sit back down and let's discuss this like rational adults." His eyes battled with hers. "Please, all I ask is for another five minutes of your time."

"Fine," she said through gritted teeth as they resumed their seats.

He leaned forward and brought his fingers to his lips, forming a steeple. Then a look of intense concentration came over his face, like he was collecting his thoughts and about to bequeath her a great gift of knowledge. She'd watched Roland go through this same routine many times, right before he delivered closing remarks to a jury. She wondered if he knew how disgustingly predictable he was.

He cleared his throat, his voice growing reflective. "I know I've made my share of mistakes. Done things I regret. But I've learned from those mistakes." His eyes met hers. "I want you to know that you and Jordan are everything to me." His voice quivered as he reached for her hand. "Everly, I love you and want us to work. Come back to me, I promise it'll be different this time."

Roland's delivery was so over-the-top that Everly felt like she was watching an actor, delivering the final lines of a play. He looked at her with puppy-dog eyes, as if he truly expected her to forgive him on the spot. She just sat there, looking at him.

"Well, say something," he said, annoyance coating his voice.

"I'm not sure what to say. You and I are divorced."

His face went slack. "But you must still feel something for me."

Her neck and shoulders were tense to the point of aching. "No, I don't." She looked him in the eye. "I'm sorry. You're a part of Jordan's life and must therefore be a part of mine. But as far as the two of us are concerned, there's nothing there. Any feelings I had for you died a long time ago when you were unfaithful the first time. Since then, there've been so many women, I've stopped counting."

He winced.

"I've got to get home."

The mask fell away as malice flashed in his eyes. "Okay, let's try this another way. There are incriminating pictures of you, plastered all over the place. It wasn't the smartest move to get tangled up with a movie star who has reporters watching his every move."

She arched an eyebrow. "I've done nothing that I'm ashamed of." What she could've added was that the few precious days she'd spent with Christian had been more real and meaningful to her than all the years she'd been married to Roland. Christian understood her in a way Roland never had, and he was a good person. A deep weariness settled over her, leaving her feeling heartsick. "I don't know why I'm even trying to explain this to you." An image of Christian with his contemplative green eyes flashed before her eyes, and she felt such a powerful longing for him that she could hardly stand it. In that moment, she had the distinct impression that she no longer belonged here in South Carolina. Christian's world—with the lush grounds and salty air—was more genuine than anything she'd ever experienced here. Fate had a funny way of showing her the truth when she least expected it. She'd been so worried that she was making a mistake with Christian—that he might not be the man she thought he was. But sitting here, face to face, with Roland the truth was painfully obvious, like comparing vinyl to supple leather.

Roland continued as if she hadn't spoken. "And if you ask me, it was rather irresponsible of you to go dilly dallying in a hot tub with some guy you'd only just met, when our son was in the house alone." He crossed his legs and adjusted the crease on his pants. His expression grew thoughtful. "Let's examine the evidence, shall we? You take Jordan to Hawaii, without my knowledge. You stay at the home of Christian Ross, whom you'd only just met. A man who, by the way, contributed to his girlfriend's paralysis and subsequent suicide. And the most damaging piece of evidence ... you leave our son alone ... in a strange home ... while you spend Christmas, frolicking in a hot tub with that man. Doesn't paint a picture of a very responsible mother."

Blood rushed to her face.

"I'm just wondering what a judge would think. Don't get me wrong. The last thing I want to do is to take you to court to get full custody of Jordan. But at the same time, I have an obligation to protect him. You and I both know that he'll be better off here, with me, where I can keep an eye on him. Of course you're welcome to stay here too," he added casually, flicking a piece of lint off his sweater.

She felt like she might have an out-of-body experience as she sprang to her feet. "You're a horrible person! Stay away from me and my son." She barged past him.

"Think about it, Everly," he called after her. "We can do this the hard way, or the easy way. Your decision."

CHAPTER 16

"Be a good boy for Momaw, okay?" Everly leaned over and kissed the top of Jordan's head before reaching for her keys and slinging her purse strap over her shoulder. She was headed to work. Normally, she dropped Jordan off at preschool on her way. However, after what happened with Roland the day before, she decided it would be safer to leave him with her mama. Florence had graciously agreed to come to Everly's house and stay with Jordan. Everly wasn't sure how long she would keep Jordan out of preschool. But right now, it seemed to be the only option. She couldn't risk Roland picking him up from school again. Next time, he might prevent her from seeing Jordan. She shuddered as his threats came rushing back. He was going to fight her for custody of Jordan. And she couldn't take a chance that he was bluffing. Her only option was to hire an attorney. But she needed to find someone outside of Roland's influence. She would have to use the money she'd been saving to invest in a fitness center to pay for it. The heaviness of the situation seemed almost too much to bear.

She paused beside Florence, who was standing at the stove making oatmeal. "Thanks again for watching Jordan."

"Honey, you don't have to keep thanking me. I'm glad to do it,"

Florence said, wiping her hands on a paper towel. "I'm only sorry you're going through such a hard time."

The sympathetic look on her mama's lined face caused tears to well in Everly's eyes. Hastily, she brushed them away. "I'll see y'all after while." She had to turn away before she completely lost it.

"Hey, I know you need to get to work, but do you have a minute?"

Everly nodded.

Florence leaned back against the counter and pushed back a strand of gray hair. Before the cancer, her hair had been the same color as Everly's, with a sprinkle of gray hairs mixed in. She'd lost it all when she had the chemo and radiation. And when it came back, it was silver. Florence decided to keep it that way for convenience. "I've been giving your situation a lot of thought, and I wonder if you're not making a mistake."

Everly tightened. "What do you mean?"

"The reason you broke things off with Christian was because you were distraught over the way the media hounded you."

Her brow creased, and she wondered where this was going. "I don't like having my personal life displayed to the world."

"And you were worried about what Roland would do." Florence gave her a probing look. "Am I right?"

"Yes." She began winding her hand around her purse strap.

"Okay, the media's hounding you now. Could it get any worse?"

Everly thought for a minute. "I'm not sure. I keep hoping that the paparazzi will grow tired of my story and move onto something else. But I know that won't happen if I get back together with Christian. I'll be hounded for the rest of my life."

"Let's talk about Roland."

At the mere mention of his name, fresh anger scoured over Everly.

"Things are already bad with him. The damage has been done. You really have only two choices—go back to him or fight."

The fire in Florence's eyes awakened the fight in Everly as she straightened to her full height. "The first choice is not an option."

Florence nodded in satisfaction. "Good."

She paused, and Everly wondered again where this was going.

Florence locked eyes with Everly. "Here's the most important question of all—do you love Christian?"

Everly was unprepared for the tumult of emotions that rolled over her.

"Do you?" Florence prodded, her steely look willing Everly to tell the truth.

"Yes, I love him." The spoken words were not only an admission to her mama, but also to herself.

"I figured you must. Otherwise, you wouldn't be so miserable."

The words settled like a steel weight on her chest. "I'm sorry, I didn't mean to come across that way."

She waved away the apology. "Love is not something you simply fall into. It has to be fought for. There are always obstacles. And you can't give up just because things are hard."

Everly swallowed hard to stay the emotion.

Florence put a hand on her shoulder. "Give the best you have, and it will never be enough. Give your best anyway."

The words burned through Everly as her head shot up. A sob started in her throat and worked its way out of her mouth. She gulped in order to choke it back down. Then the dam broke. She threw her arms around her mama and began to cry.

Everly was sitting at her desk, trying to work out the new fitness schedule for the instructors when a knock sounded on her office door. She looked up as Jessica the Zumba and spinning class instructor stuck her head in the door.

"Hey," she said. "Have you been online in the last hour?"

Everly's throat went dry. "No. What's going on?" She braced herself for the answer. There was no telling what the media had put up about her this time.

"I think you'd better take a look."

Dread churned in Everly's stomach. "Okay," she said, trying to keep her expression passive, even though she felt shaky. "What site is it?"

Jessica came around the desk. "Here, I'll show you." Everly scooted back her chair, so Jessica could get to the keyboard. A minute later, she pulled up an interview with well-known Katie Moss from CBS. And then Everly realized Katie was interviewing Christian! He was wearing jeans and a black t-shirt that emphasized his muscular biceps and pecs. A dart of warmth shot through Everly. Seeing him again made the pain of losing him so sharp she felt it in her chest.

"Thanks for joining me today," Katie began.

Christian smiled. "I'm glad to be here."

From what Everly could tell, it looked like they were in the living room of a hotel room. Was Katie in Hawaii? Or had Christian gone to her?

"To start our interview, I've got to ask the one thing viewers will want to know. Are you going to do another Jase Scott movie?"

He looked thoughtful. "Let's just say I'm considering it."

That was certainly news to Everly.

"Ooh, I hope you do," Katie gushed. "That's such a great series. Few actors are as successful as you."

For the first time, Christian looked uncomfortable. "I love making movies. It's what I do."

"And you do it well," she purred, touching his arm. " I understand you do all of your own stunts."

"Yes. It helps me connect on a personal level with the character."

Katie's voice grew businesslike as she switched gears. "There's been a great deal of controversy surrounding your recent relationship with Everly Watson. Can you tell me about that?"

"Certainly. I met Everly and her son Jordan when they came to Hawaii on vacation."

Katie stopped him. "It is my understanding that Everly went to Hawaii searching for information on a former husband who was presumed dead."

Everly clasped her hands together tightly, waiting to see how he would respond.

"Yes, she was seeking information about him, but she was also on vacation."

"How did you meet?"

A crooked smile formed over his lips. "We were both at the beach. I ran out of sun block, so I asked to borrow hers."

Katie laughed. "How very fortunate for her."

He grinned. "And for me."

Rosiness spread over Everly's cheeks, and she could feel Jessica's watchful eyes on her.

Katie continued. "So the two of you formed an attachment and started a relationship?"

"Yes, that's the shortened version." Christian told about the tsunami threat and how he'd taken Everly and Jordan to his home for safety. Then he outlined how they'd ended up staying with him.

"Let's talk about the pictures taken of the two of you in the hot tub on Christmas."

Everly held her breath, waiting for his response.

"After Everly put Jordan to bed, I suggested that we go for a swim. That ended in the hot tub. Everly didn't want to leave Jordan alone, but I assured her he would be fine. I brought out a baby monitor that I sometimes use when my niece stays over. We took it to the pool, so we could hear if he needed anything."

"I see."

"Everly's a great person." His voice grew affectionate. "She's warm and open, and I feel blessed to know her," he finished, looking directly into the camera. Everly had the impression he was looking straight at her.

"It sounds like you're very fond of her."

"Oh, it's more than fondness. I'll say it straight out. I'm in love with her."

Katie was surprised. "That's a bold statement."

Christian placed his hands together. "Katie, there's very little about my life that the media doesn't already know. So, I figure I might as well say it myself and save on the speculation."

The stinger found its mark as Katie laughed nervously. "Sounds reasonable, I suppose."

He cleared his throat. "As you know, I went through a difficult time when my former girlfriend, Heather, passed away." He hesitated. "There aren't any instruction manuals for that kind of thing. One minute you're living your life, and the next, everything falls apart. I ..." He stopped, his eyes filling with pain. "I shut down ... stopped acting ... stopped living ... mainly just existed, you know?"

She gave him a sympathetic nod.

"Everly helped me find my purpose again. She brought light back into my life."

Everly couldn't stop the tears from streaming down her face.

"Why her?"

"That was a rude thing to say," Jessica said, frowning.

Christian rubbed his jaw. "Because ever since I've met her, she's all I can think about." He laughed. "I love the stubborn glint in her eyes when she's irritated. The way her hair falls on her shoulders. Her adorable southern accent. How she can give me a good tongue-lashing when the situation warrants it. I love that she's such a good mother to Jordan, always putting him first, even if it means sacrificing what she wants."

"Interesting. What do you mean by that?"

He shook his head. "Everly knows what I mean," he said quietly.

Katie eyed him. "Let's talk about regrets. Do you have any?"

"Who doesn't," he said dryly.

She offered him a courtesy smile. "Point taken." She leaned forward slightly, honing in for the kill. "But I want to hear about your regrets."

Irritation crawled up Everly's neck. Why was she hounding him? Was she trying to get him to publicly admit that he regretted the accident and Heather's death?

Christian looked thoughtful. "My biggest regret of late is that my relationship with Everly caused her to come under public scrutiny. She's a good person and doesn't deserve that." He looked into the camera. "I will be forever grateful for her, because she gave me the courage to start living my life again. And Everly ..." he paused, a ghost of a smile on his lips "... no matter what happens from here on out, I want you to know that I love you anyway."

"Well, that's just about the sweetest thing I've ever heard," Jessica cooed.

Everly looked straight ahead, tears brimming in her eyes.

CHAPTER 17

When Everly returned home, she found her mama sitting on the sofa, a strange expression on her face.

Her stomach rolled as she looked around wildly. "Where's Jordan?"

"He's fine."

Relief pulsed over her. "Where is he?"

"Outside. Playing catch."

It was a cold, overcast day. Certainly not the best day to be outside playing. She thought her mama had better judgment than to allow him to do that. "Did he wear a coat?"

Florence nodded. "Of course." She smiled and patted the spot beside her. "Sit down. I want to talk to you."

Everly removed her coat and placed it on the table. "Is everything okay?" Her mama was acting really strange.

"Yes, it's fine, dear."

Everly sat down beside her. Florence took a deep breath. "Did you see Christian's interview today?"

"Yes, but how did you know about it?"

"Charlotte called and told me to watch it." Her eyes started shining. "He really loves you, doesn't he?"

A lump formed in Everly's throat. "Yes."

She shifted uncomfortably. "I hope you're not upset ..." She began chewing on her lower lip as she glanced toward the patio.

Everly looked in the same direction, not seeing anything amiss. "What's going on?"

Florence squeezed her hand. She looked like she was going to say something but then changed her mind and stood. "Let's go outside."

Her mama's odd behavior was perplexing and a little irritating. Everly knitted her brows. "Tell me what's happening!" She was already stretched to the limit emotionally and couldn't handle anything else.

"It's better if I just show you." She motioned. "Come on."

"Fine," she huffed. When they stepped through the patio door, into the backyard, Everly couldn't believe what she was seeing. She gasped, her hand covering her mouth. Christian was pitching a ball to Jordan. When Jordan saw her, he began jumping up and down. "Look, Mommy, I caught the ball." He raised it high in the air.

Everly was at a loss for words. She just stood there, her feet rooted to the ground until Florence nudged her. "Go on. Talk to him."

Christian met her halfway. "Hey," he said tentatively.

"Hey," she said quietly as blood pumped furiously through her veins. "You're here." She had to speak the words out loud in order to believe it.

A smile stole over his lips. "Yeah, I figured it was time to get off the island and do a little something with my life."

She matched his smile. "It's about time." A bubble of pleasure burst over her as her heart sprouted wings. He'd come for her! That meant more than words could express. "I saw your interview."

"Oh, yeah?"

She stepped into his personal space and put a hand on his chest. "Yeah." She pressed her lips together, studying him critically. "You do look a little smaller in person though," she teased.

His eyes danced. "Is that right."

Her breath caught when he encircled her waist and pulled her close. He leaned over her, arching her back, an intense look on his beautiful face. "I love you, Everly," he murmured in her ear.

"I love you too."

He pulled back, cautious hope in his eyes. "Really?"

"Really," she said decisively, leaving zero room for doubt.

"That's wonderful news," he uttered, passion darkening his eyes as he leaned in. A surge ran through her as his lips touched hers. She slipped her arms around his neck and pulled him close, wanting as much of him as she could get. Being with him was like breathing the purest oxygen and seeing clearly, whereas before she'd been floundering in stale air, slowly suffocating. He would've given her a longer kiss had her mama not awkwardly cleared her throat.

Jordan wrinkled his nose. "Ew ... kissing is gross."

"You won't feel that way one day," Everly said.

Christian chuckled. "Amen."

Jordan skipped over and tugged on Christian's arm. "Come and pitch to me."

It warmed Everly's heart to see Jordan this excited about Christian's arrival. Both of them, it seemed, needed Christian in their lives.

Christian and Jordan picked up where they'd left off before Everly and Florence came outside.

Everly and her mama sat down at a nearby table. Florence turned to Everly. "It looks like you've finally found your match." She patted Everly's hand. "I guess the third time really is the charm."

A few minutes later, Christian approached the table and sat down beside Everly. He pulled his coat tighter around him, shaking off a shiver. "It's cold."

Everly looked up at the sky and the clouds rumbling above. Funny. It didn't seem nearly as ominous and bleak to her now as it had thirty minutes ago. Now that Christian was here, everything was brighter. A sense of renewed energy flowed through her, and she felt like she could sprint a mile. The wind picked up. This time, she shivered. It had been hard for Everly to come back to winter after being in Hawaii. She could imagine how Christian must feel, since his body was acclimated to the heat. "You're not in Kansas anymore, Toto," she teased.

"Or Hawaii," Christian added with a laugh.

"We can go inside, if you want," Everly said.

"I'm alright," Christian said, adopting a tough-guy tone. "I like turning into an ice cube."

Everly laughed.

They sat there for a minute, until Everly turned to him. "I still can't believe you're here." Her eyes went soft as she placed a hand over his. "All of those things you said in the interview. Thank you."

"I only spoke the truth." He winked. "And you love me anyway. Proof that miracles still happen."

Florence giggled. "I knew I liked you ... the minute you started quoting my poem on TV."

Christian gave Florence a grateful smile, revealing his dimple. "You're the mastermind. Thank you."

Florence looked surprised and then a hint of adoration touched her features. "You're welcome."

Everly smiled inwardly. It had taken less than an hour for Christian to win her mama over. Then again, she couldn't say much. It'd taken mere days for him to win her heart. *Like mama, like daughter.*

Silence stretched between them and Florence stood. "I think I'll get dinner started."

Everly smiled inwardly as she thought of something her mama often said, *A true lady always knows when to leave the conversation.*

"Your mom's great," Christian said as they watched her go into the house.

"Yes, she is." Everly shifted, trying to find a way to voice the question that formed in her mind the minute she saw Christian in the backyard with Jordan. "So, where do we go from here?"

Christian looked thoughtful. "Wherever we want."

"Hmm ... I kind of like the idea of running a fitness center in Hawaii."

"Me too."

"But what about your movie? Are you really considering it?"

"Yes." Excitement coated his voice. "How do you feel about spending part of the year in L.A.?"

"As long as we're together, I'm good with it." The past week without him had been agonizing. She never wanted to go through that again. She linked her arm through his and snuggled closer, not wanting to let him out of her reach. They watched Jordan play on the swing-set until Christian spoke. "There's something important I need to tell you." He looked at her. "It's about the paparazzi."

She scowled. "It's been brutal."

He nodded. "I know. And I'm truly sorry my career has caused you grief."

She shrugged. "Every couple has something they have to work through, albeit ours is a little more extreme. But we'll work our way through it ..." she gave him a meaningful look "... together."

He appraised her. "You're really something."

She loved the feeling of belonging that flooded through her when he stroked her hair.

Her intense attraction to him was getting her off track. She went back to something he'd said earlier. "What do you need to talk to me about?"

His eyes grew troubled. "When we were in Hawaii, having issues with Briggs, I hired a Private Investigator to look into Roland."

Her eyes widened.

"I wanted to see what we were up against."

She nodded. "I don't blame you one bit. What did you find out?"

He hesitated.

"Tell me," she prompted.

"Roland is the one behind the media frenzy."

She gasped, clutching her throat. "Are you sure?"

"Yes, the P.I. did some digging and discovered that Roland paid Bart, the reporter for *Introspective Magazine*, to spin a negative slant on the story. Of course, it probably didn't take much convincing because I brushed Bart off."

Blood shot to Everly's face, and she had the urge to rip Roland's head off. "I should've known," she muttered. "This is a new low ... even for him."

"The pictures in the tabloids weren't taken by Bart, however. They were taken by Briggs."

It all came together in one hard slap. "No wonder the media was so concerned about Jordan's whereabouts while we were in the hot tub." Fury coursed through her as she clenched her fists. "Roland's trying to cast me as irresponsible. That way, he can keep me in line— use the constant threat of taking Jordan away as a weapon. He outright told me yesterday that he is going to take me to court and get full custody of Jordan. Of course, he added that all of my problems would go away if I agreed to get back together with him." The whole thing was nauseatingly disgusting.

Fury swept over Christian's face. "That's not going to happen. I don't care how much it costs, we'll fight him."

"Thank you," Everly said hoarsely, trying to keep her emotions in check. "But we will be hard pressed to find an attorney in South Carolina, who's not influenced by Roland."

He tilted his head, considering her words. "You're absolutely right."

Her heart dropped. "I am?"

"Yes, we would have a hard time finding someone in South Carolina ... but not in Hawaii or California."

"I suppose that's true." She told Christian how Roland had picked Jordan up from school without her knowledge. A sharp fear sliced through her. "As grateful as I am that you're here, I fear what Roland might do when he finds out. Not only does he have connections in the courts, but also in the police department."

"Okay, then we need to leave for Hawaii immediately."

"What?" Could she really just pack up and leave?

"If you wait until Roland gets wind of you leaving, then he'll try and stop you. But at this moment, he doesn't even realize I'm in town."

"Or that we're back together. It could work." The prospect was exciting and a little scary. She'd never just picked up and left a place before. Her boss Matt would be livid ... or maybe not. He'd been so disgruntled about the press thing that he might be relieved.

"I'll hire a security team to watch the estate." Regret tinged his features. "Had I done that earlier, we wouldn't be in this mess."

"Don't beat yourself up. As ruthless as Roland is, he would've found a way to undermine our relationship. No matter what."

Marbles appeared at the corners of his jaw. "Well, he'll have a much harder time getting to you there, than here."

Everly ran through various scenarios. Christian was right. The best way to outwit Roland was to act quickly. Life really was opening up a golden nugget of possibility, but she had to summon the courage to take hold. She took a deep breath. "Okay, let's do it."

CHAPTER 18

Everly sat by the pool, enjoying the soothing sound of the waterfall flowing over the rocks. A light breeze ruffled her hair as she breathed in the scent of flowers. It had been exactly one week since they'd left South Carolina and taken a red-eye flight to Hawaii. The past week had been surprisingly peaceful, considering how worried she was about Roland.

She'd left her old phone at her home in South Carolina, just in case Roland was tracking it. The day after they arrived in Hawaii, Christian bought her a new phone. At which point, she called her mama and gave her the number. Even though Everly and Christian invited Florence to come with them, she decided to stay in South Carolina a while longer. Everly was relieved when Florence told her she was going to Greenville for a few months to live with her sister before coming to spend a few months in Hawaii with them. She didn't want her mama in close proximity to Roland, for fear of what he might do.

A part of her wondered what Matt and the employees at the fitness center thought when she simply didn't show up for work. She hated leaving them in the lurch, but it couldn't be helped. There was still her house to consider. She didn't want it sitting empty for a long period of time. Christian suggested they hire someone to pack up her personal items, place them in storage, and then put the home on the market. The more she thought about it, that seemed to be the most feasible option.

Christian came up behind her and began massaging her shoulders. "I wondered where you'd gotten off to. How ya doing?"

"Great." Her senses seemed to come alive at his touch. "You have magic hands," she murmured. "You're distracting me."

He chuckled. "That's the idea. What ya working on?"

She motioned at the laptop on the poolside table. "Just strategizing for the fitness center." They'd already looked for property on which to build the center and found the perfect spot in Haleiwa. They put in an offer, and it was accepted twenty-four hours later. Everything seemed to be falling into place in record time

Christian leaned in, and she inhaled his clean, masculine scent that smelled of cinnamon. "You've been drinking hot chocolate."

"Want some?"

"Maybe later."

He leaned in and placed a string of light kisses down her neck. Every cell in her body came alive with a spiral of pleasure. The need for him consumed her as she turned to kiss him full on the mouth. He pulled her to her feet and encircled her in his arms. She ran her hands along his arms, appreciating his defined muscles. Her lips parted expectantly as he moved closer. When their mouths connected, a flame ignited between them. Their lips moved in perfect sync and they melted into each other. They only pulled apart for want of air.

"It just keeps getting better and better," Christian said fiercely.

"Agreed." She'd never before been this happy, but she couldn't help feeling this was the calm before the storm. They'd hired an attorney to represent her, and he kept assuring Everly that everything would be fine, but she was worried. Roland was a force to be reckoned with, and he wouldn't stop until he destroyed her.

Concern touched his features. "What's wrong?"

"I just keep feeling like something bad is about to happen. I worry what Roland will do."

"You need to stop," he said firmly. "Everything will be okay."

She nodded but couldn't shake the sick feeling in her gut. They sat down in the lounge chairs, and she snuggled close to Christian. "Any news about the movie?"

"Still in negotiation."

She thrust out her lower lip in a pout. "I'm not sure how I feel about you kissing another woman."

A mischievous smile flittered over his lips. "It's just acting. It doesn't mean anything."

"Bull crap."

His eyes widened, and he burst out laughing. "You really are something. You could always be my co-star."

She cut her eyes at him. "Yeah, right."

"I'm sure you could act."

She batted her eyelashes alluringly. "Well, I can certainly do a convincing Scarlett O'Hara."

"Really?"

"Sure can. I played her in my senior high school play."

He grinned. "This I've gotta see."

She paused. "Let's see if I can remember the lines. She sat up straight in her chair. "Oh, Rhett!" she gushed, bringing her hands together. "When I think of myself ... with anything I could possibly hope for," she chirped, flouncing her hair, "not a care in the world ..." she adopted a petulant frown "... and you here in this horrid jail." She balled her fist. "And not even a human jail, Rhett, a horse jail," she wailed, letting out a long sigh. Then she hiccupped a self-deprecating laugh. "Listen to me trying to make jokes, when I really wanna cry." She fluttered her eyelashes, adopting a glib expression. "In a minute ... I think I will cry."

He started clapping. "That's pretty good ... for an amateur."

"What?" She shoved him. "I thought that was pretty convincing."

Amusement danced in his eyes. "Well, you certainly have the Southern accent pegged. But maybe you'd better stick to running a fitness center and leave the acting to me." He started tickling her. She jumped back, "St-op," she laughed.

A few minutes later, he scooted his chair closer and they cuddled up.

"Show me what you've got for the fitness center," he said.

She could tell that he genuinely wanted to know, and that thrilled her to the core. "Okay, here's what I was thinking ..."

Everly was weightless and free, moving through the water as she and Mitchell explored the shipwreck. Time was distorted underwater, but Everly was certain they'd been under too long. She kept pointing towards the surface, shining like the moon in the blue abyss. She tried to persuade Mitchell to go up with her. But he shook his head *no* and took off in another direction. She went after him, but as soon as she got close enough to touch him, he darted out of her grasp. Fearing for her own safety, she started going up and then realized Mitchell was struggling. In a flurry, she went back down to help him. His eyes radiated panic through the mask. He was running out of air! She tried help, but it was no use. Anguish wrenched her gut as she watched him sink into the black nothingness. Then it occurred to her that this was a dream, and she had the power to change it. She used all of her concentration to exert her will. At that moment, she saw Christian above her, holding out his hand. As she clutched it, they zoomed, side-by-side, to the surface.

Her eyes popped open as a hand pressed over her mouth. Panic raced through Everly as she looked at the face looming over her. Christian! He put a finger to his lips. "Someone's in the house," he whispered.

Sleep immediately fled as Everly tossed off the covers and leapt out of bed. Sweat broke over her brow as she thought of Jordan, sleeping in the room at the end of the hall. "We have to get to Jordan," she whispered.

Christian nodded.

They heard a slight creaking noise and both went statue still, craning their ears to hear.

Christian had already hired a couple of guards to watch the grounds and had ordered a security system, but it was scheduled to be installed two days from now.

Everly's heart was in her throat as they inched to the door of her bedroom. Every step on the wood floor seemed to crack like a gunshot in the still house. Christian looked out into the hallway. "The coast is clear," he whispered.

She caught his arm. "What happened?"

"I was asleep when I heard a noise," he whispered. "I came to your door to check on you, then I heard someone walking downstairs. That's when I woke you up."

Everly's pulse hammered in her ears as she nodded. Stealthily, they made their way to Jordan's room. When they heard a muffled sound, they ran to the door. Christian threw it open, and Everly flipped on the light.

She cried out when she saw Roland, holding a sleeping Jordan in his arms. She rushed forward. "Put him down!" Then she saw the glint of metal and realized Roland was pointing a gun.

"Stop where you are," he ordered.

A swift terror rushed over her as she complied, holding up her hands. She felt movement from behind as Christian stepped up beside her.

"I said stop," Roland thundered, a crazed look in his eyes.

Jordan opened his eyes. "Daddy?"

Roland forced a smile. "Hey, buddy."

Jordan looked around and saw Everly. He tried to wiggle out of Roland's arms, but Roland held him tight.

"I want my mommy!" Tears erupted as his face crumbled into sobs.

Everly felt her own eyes grow moist. "Roland, please, put him down. Let's talk about this rationally."

"Rationally?" He let out a grating laugh. "I tried to handle the situation rationally. Called you to my home. Gave you the opportunity to come back, but you wouldn't do it." His voice broke. "You betrayed me, Everly. And now, I'm taking my son home where he belongs."

Panic filled Jordan's eyes. "No! I want to stay here with Mommy and Christian."

"Shut up," Roland barked.

Everly winced as rage contorted Roland's features. This was her worst fear, coming to life. Sheer desperation overcame Everly as she looked at Jordan. It was all she could do to keep her voice even. "Do what he says, okay?"

"Put Jordan down," Christian demanded through clenched teeth.

Everly noticed out of the corner of her eye that Christian had inched up a couple of steps. His body was pulled taut, a panther ready to pounce.

Roland's eyes turned to icy flecks as he glared at Christian. "You're the one to blame for this entire thing."

Things were spiraling out of control. Instinct told Everly that if she allowed Roland to walk out of this house with Jordan, she would never see her son again. She would do everything in her power to protect Jordan, even if it meant dying in the process. Frantically, she searched her brain for a way to appease Roland. "I'll go with you," she blurted. "I will," she said, holding Roland's eyes. She could almost see the cogs in his brain churning as he considered what she'd said. "Both of us can take Jordan home. Just put him down. You're scaring him."

Roland sneered. "Do you think I'm stupid?"

"No, I don't think you're stupid at all," Everly continued. "I think you're upset." And then she had an idea. What they needed was a distraction. She glanced at Christian, wishing he could read her mind. "If you wanna know the truth, I'm glad you're here." She jutted her thumb in Christian's direction. "Because I've just about had enough of this puffed-up, pretty-boy actor who's been strutting around like a peacock. I guess my mama was right when she said, 'Never date a guy prettier than you.'"

Christian jerked, stunned. "What?"

She slapped him hard across the face. "It's like I told you earlier by the pool. I shouldn't have come here. We're from two different worlds. It's not working. You're an actor, for goodness sakes! How can I believe a word you say? I told you it wouldn't work, but you dragged me here anyway."

For a second, Christian just stood there, dumbfounded, as she silently tried to convey what she was doing. "Say something," she demanded, shoving him hard in the chest. "I said you dragged me here anyway! This place is worse than a jail!"

Suddenly, it clicked as he got up in her face. "How dare you say those things to me. You're lucky I even gave you the time of day."

Everly went wild, rushing at Christian, attacking him for all she was worth.

"Hey!" Roland yelled. He put Jordan down on the bed and then turned to them. "I said enough!"

Jordan was whimpering, his eyes filled with fear.

Everly stumbled and fell forward into Roland. When he moved to help break her fall, Christian charged at him full force, knocking the gun out of his hands. Everly scrambled to get it, while the two men crashed into the nearby bookshelf. They rolled on the floor, trading blows. But the fight was over quickly when Christian flipped Roland over, face-first on the floor and thrust his knee into his back, pinning him to the ground.

Everly handed Christian the gun. He jabbed it into the center of Roland's back.

"On your feet," he ordered. Then he looked at Everly. "Call 911."

Roland shot Everly a venomous look. "You think you're so smart. But you'll pay dearly for that."

Christian shook his head, a look of revulsion coming over him. "She's already paid dearly for all the crap you've put her through. Now it's your turn to pay. And if I have anything to do with it, you'll be paying for your sins for a very long time."

Everly returned a couple of minutes later. "The police are on the way." She hurried to Jordan's side and gathered him in her arms. He buried his head in her chest. She could only hope the night's events wouldn't leave him scarred.

She glanced at Roland one final time. Even though he wore a surly expression, his shoulders sagged in defeat. He seemed puny in comparison to Christian. She knew enough about the law to know that thanks to this escapade, he would be charged with enough crimes to keep him on the defensive for quite some time. And he would most likely serve jail time. No amount of influence on his part could convince a judge to grant him full custody of Jordan.

Christian's eyes connected with hers. "Are you okay?"

She gave him a weak smile. "Yeah." For the first time, she really was.

After the police took Roland away, Everly laid down beside Jordan, until he drifted off to sleep. Then she joined Christian in the living room for a cup of hot chocolate. He'd turned on music, and it was playing in the background. Christian turned to her, a slow grin crossing his face. "I guess I stand corrected."

She took a drink from her cup and placed it on the coffee table. "What do you mean?"

"You're a pretty good actress ... for an amateur."

"Uh, huh. I hear ya."

He placed his cup beside hers. "Seriously, for a minute there, I wasn't sure what was going on when you went all Rosie O' Donnell on me. But when you mentioned the word *jail*, it clicked."

She flashed a coquettish smile. "Not just any jail, Rhett ... but a horse jail," she drawled.

He put an arm around her. "So you're a fitness expert, an amazing cook, a tolerably good actress." He winked. "Tell me, Everly, Southern Belle extraordinaire—is there anything you can't do?"

She thought for a second. "Live without you."

Her forthright answer caught him off guard, and she thought she might've seen a tear form in his eye, but he blinked it away. Then a radiant smile touched his lips. "Hey, they're playing our song." He began singing along softly to the lyrics.

She had so much to be grateful for and could hardly believe she was here, in this beautiful place, with the love of her life. Everly trailed a hand along the line of Christian's jaw, her voice growing reflective. "Despite all of the heartache the two of us have endured, it really is a wonderful world anyway."

His eyes captured hers, and she thought she might've caught a glimpse of eternity as he clasped his hand over hers. "Yes, and what a wonderful world it is."

Want more Hawaii Billionaire Romance? Check out *Love at the Ocean Breeze*, the next book in the series.

EXCERPT OF LOVE AT THE OCEAN BREEZE (HAWAII BILLIONAIRE ROMANCE)

Lacey's stomach growled. If only she'd thought to pack a granola bar … or something to snack on. She and Milo had been trudging through the overgrown trail for over an hour. She'd drained her water bottle in the first twenty minutes of the hike, and a blister was forming where the strap of her sandal rubbed relentlessly against her heel. *Why had she not thought to wear tennis shoes?* "Can we please turn around and go back?" she asked wearily.

Not bothering to look at her, Milo waved a hand as he increased his pace. "The waterfall's great, babe. There's a pool below it where we can swim. We're almost there. Just a little further."

"That's what you said thirty minutes ago," she grumbled, hurrying to keep up. Milo had grown up in the nearby town of Hauula, Hawaii. But he hadn't been to this waterfall since he was a kid. Even though he swore he knew the way, Lacey was starting to wonder. At this point, she didn't give a flying flip about some waterfall —no matter how beautiful it was. But Milo was determined to forge on until he found it or they passed out from exhaustion. And judging from the way things were going, it would most assuredly be the latter.

Lacey swatted the mosquito on her leg. She managed to kill that one, but ten more took its place in the blink of an eye. She was getting eaten alive! The air oozed moisture, bathing her in sticky sweat. If only her Texas friends could see her now. She glanced at the waist-high weeds and vines growing in tangles, and the trees crowding in around them. It looked like a scene straight out of *The Jungle Book*. She chuckled humorlessly at the thought. She'd come to Hawaii three months ago on vacation. Her second day on the island, she met Milo Kahele at Waimea Bay where he was back diving off a cliff. He was a local boy—a surfer heartthrob with a quick smile and great body. They'd been inseparable ever since. Her older brother Trevor didn't approve of the relationship and would freak if he knew she was living with Milo. Trevor was always calling and texting, trying to get her to come back home and enroll in a community college. But it was none of his stinking business what she did with her life. She was an adult and could do as she pleased. She had no intention of sitting in a boring classroom. She'd never had as much fun with anyone as she had with Milo ... well, most of the time, present activity excluded. Her lips formed a petulant scowl. If Milo didn't find the wretched water-fall soon, she was going back to the house—with or without him.

Milo stopped so suddenly that Lacey nearly toppled forward to avoid barreling into him. "Careful," she growled.

Milo stepped into a clearing, and Lacey followed close behind. For a split second, she thought he might've actually found the water-fall, but no—it was only a crummy building that looked like it had been forgotten eons ago.

"I could've sworn we were going the right way," Milo said, scratching his head.

"Obviously not," she retorted, blowing out a long breath. "We need to go back. I have a blister on my foot." She looked at her heel. It was bleeding. Where was a Band-Aid when she needed it?

His shoulders sagged in defeat. "Okay."

Lacey plopped down on the ground. "I need to rest a minute before we head back." She groaned. It felt good to sit down. "Care to join me?"

"Yeah," he said absently, his eyes darting to the shack. "A strange place for a building."

"I guess." Lacey stretched out her legs, her stomach growling again. "Do you have any snacks in your backpack?"

"No, sorry. I think I'm gonna check it out."

Her face fell. "What? The building? No." She pointed. "There's a padlock on the door. That's code for *keep out*."

"Nah, dat means there's something valuable inside."

"Yeah, spiders and bugs."

He wriggled his eyebrows, an adventurous smile curving his lips. "Be right back."

"I don't think that's a good idea," Lacey said, but he was already jogging towards the building.

Milo tugged on the padlock. When it didn't budge, Lacey assumed he'd grow tired of the game and come back. To her dismay, Milo found a rock and beat on the lock. A couple of minutes later, it broke. Milo pushed open the door and stepped inside.

Lacey tensed, glancing around. Even though it looked forgotten, the building belonged to someone. And the owner certainly wouldn't appreciate Milo breaking into it. Milo was a daredevil from the word *go*, which is what attracted her to him. But this was going too far. She stood.

"Milo," she called, "you've had your fun. It's time to go."

No answer.

"Milo!" she said angrily, rushing toward the building.

Before Lacey got to the door, Milo came running out, a look of exhilaration on his face. "You won't believe it. The whole building's filled with crates of paintings and statues."

"Whatever's in there, doesn't belong to us. We need to go."

He let out a loud whoop. "Ever heard of *finders keepers*? This is incredible, babe." He took her hand. "Come on. I'll show you. The stuff looks expensive."

Lacey picked through the crate closest to the door. It didn't take a trained professional to know that Milo was right. The paintings were exquisitely done in vivid detail. The items were valuable.

"We can sell these." He began talking fast. "One piece will probably bring more money than we could make in a year." He laughed. "Ten years." He clenched a fist. "Oh, my gosh. I can't believe it!"

"I don't know." Lacey chewed on her cheek. "These pieces belong to someone. They'll come back for them. Maybe they're stolen."

Milo grabbed her arms, a feverish excitement in his eyes. "There aren't any car tracks leading to the building. And the lock was so old and rusted that all I had to do was barely hit it and it fell off. This is our lucky day. Think about it," he said enticingly. "No more waiting tables, for you. We can eat at the best restaurants. Stay in nice hotels. Maybe even buy a house."

It was tempting. Everything in Hawaii cost a fortune. Lacey had blown through her meager savings in the first week and had taken a waitress job at a café, which paid barely enough to cover her food and other expenses. Thankfully, Milo was letting her stay at his place rent free, but that couldn't last forever. Eventually, she'd have to start paying her fair share. And she couldn't do that on what she was making now. "But what'll happen if somebody finds out we took these things?" A shudder ran through her as she glanced around, looking for cameras. "What if the place is under surveillance?"

He nodded. "You're right. We need to be careful. I have a friend we can call. Someone who can help."

"A friend?" She shook her head. "I dunno. Maybe we should just walk away and pretend we never found this."

"Turn our backs on a fortune?" He squared his jaw. "We'll never get another chance like this." His eyes battled hers. "Please? Just let me call my friend."

"Okay," she finally said.

A smile broke over his lips. "You won't regret it. We're gonna be rich!"

YOUR FREE BOOK AWAITS ...

Hey there, thanks for taking the time to read *Love on the Rebound*. If you enjoyed it, please take a minute to give me a review on Amazon. I really appreciate your feedback, as I depend largely on word of mouth to promote my books.

To receive updates when more of my books are coming out, sign up for my newsletter at jenniferyoungblood.com

If you sign up for my newsletter, as a thank-you gift, I'll give you one of my books, Beastly Charm: A contemporary retelling of beauty & the beast, for FREE. Plus, you'll get information on discounts and other freebies.

Your free book awaits …

OTHER BOOKS BY JENNIFER YOUNGBLOOD

Check out Jennifer's Amazon Page.

Romeo Family Romance

One Perfect Day

One Way Home

One Little Switch

One Tiny Lie

One Big Mistake

One Southern Cowboy

One Singing Bachelorette

One Fake Fiancé

One Silent Night

One Kick Wonder

One More Chance

Billionaire Boss Romance

Her Blue Collar Boss

Her Lost Chance Boss

Georgia Patriots Romance

The Hot Headed Patriot

The Twelfth Hour Patriot

The Unstoppable Patriot

The Exiled Patriot

O'Brien Family Romance

The Impossible Groom (Chas O'Brien)

The Twelfth Hour Patriot (McKenna O'Brien)

The Stormy Warrior (Caden O'Brien and Tess Eisenhart)

Christmas

Rewriting Christmas (A Novella)

Yours By Christmas (Park City Firefighter Romance)

Her Crazy Rich Fake Fiancé

Her Christmas Wedding Fake Fiancé

Navy SEAL Romance

The Resolved Warrior

The Reckless Warrior

The Diehard Warrior

The Stormy Warrior

The Jane Austen Pact

Seeking Mr. Perfect

Texas Titan Romances

The Hometown Groom

The Persistent Groom

The Ghost Groom

The Jilted Billionaire Groom

The Impossible Groom

Hawaii Billionaire Series

Love Him or Lose Him

Love on the Rocks

Love on the Rebound

Love at the Ocean Breeze

Love Changes Everything

Loving the Movie Star

Love Under Fire (A Companion book to the Hawaii Billionaire Series)

Kisses and Commitment Series

How to See With Your Heart

Angel Matchmaker Series

Kisses Over Candlelight

The Cowboy and the Billionaire's Daughter

Romantic Thrillers

False Identity

False Trust

Promise Me Love

Burned

Contemporary Romance

Beastly Charm

Fairytale Retellings (The Grimm Laws Series)

Banish My Heart **(This book is FREE)**

The Magic in Me

Under Your Spell

A Love So True

Southern Romance

Livin' in High Cotton

Recipe for Love

The Secret Song of the Ditch Lilies

Short Stories

The Southern Fried Fix

Falling for the Doc Series (Co-authored with Craig Depew, MD)

Cooking with the Doc

Dancing with the Doc

Cruising with the Doc

Jackson Hole Firefighter Romance Series

Saving the Billionaire's Daughter

Saving His Heart (Co-authored with Agnes Canestri)

Saving Grace (Co-authored with Amelia C. Adams)

Saving the Rookie (Co-authored with Stephanie Fowers)

Saving the Captain (Co-authored with Jewel Allen)

Saving Forever (Co-authored with Shanna Delaney)

The St. Claire Sisters Series

Meet Me in London (Co-authored with Haley Hopkins)

Collections

A Merry Christmas Romance Collection
A Christmas to Remember Romance Collection
The Christmas Bliss Romance Collection
Christmas Romance Collection
The Cozy Fire Collection
Sweet Beginnings Series Starter Collection
Jennifer's Military Romance Collection
The Heart and Soul Collection
Texas Titan Romance Collection
Hawaii Billionaire Romance Collection
The Southern Romance Collection
The Romance Suspense Collection
The Originals Collection
The Spring Dream Collection
Forever Yours Collection

ABOUT THE AUTHORS

Jennifer grew up in rural Alabama and loved living in a town where "everybody knows everybody." Her love for writing began as a young teenager when she wrote stories for her high school English teacher to critique.

Jennifer has a BA in English and Social Sciences from Brigham Young University Hawaii where she served as Miss BYU Hawaii. Before becoming an author, she worked as the owner and editor of a monthly newspaper named *The Senior Times*.

She now lives in the Rocky Mountains with her family and spends her time writing and doing all of the wonderful things that make up the life of a busy wife and mother.

Sandra grew up in a small community in northeast Alabama called Alder Springs, the setting of Sandra and Jennifer's first novel, Livin' in High Cotton. It was there that she developed a deep love for literature in a two-classroom country school. She recalls that every afternoon the teachers would bring their classes together and read such classics as *Rip Van Winkle, Moby Dick, The Headless Horsemen*, and The *Taming of the Shrew* while all their students sat on the floor.

Sandra has worked in the administrative field for over twenty-five years. She worked her way through college while her daughters were very young and completed a four-year degree in three years. Later, she earned a Masters in Business Administration. Her experience has ranged from being an executive secretary and human resource manager for Fortune 500 companies to being an assistant to one of the vice presidents at the university where she eventually retired. She now works in the education field.

For Sandra, writing is a continual journey of discovery. She has so many ideas for other books running through her mind that it's hard to focus on one at a time.

Made in United States
Orlando, FL
13 August 2023

36041567R00109